WOMEN OF CHOICE
A Collection of Monologues

DAVID RUSH

OnStage Press

WOMEN OF CHOICE: A Collection of Monologues

This is for Wayne, who brought them to completion;

and for Tammy, who brought them to life.

Choices

Introduction vii

Prologue 1

Gail, the Mother 5
Mary, the Widow 6
Nancy, the Wife 7
Ariadne, the Spinner 9
Doris, the Star 11
Michelle, the Soldier 20
Aphrodite, the Street Lady 22
Minerva, the Teacher 24
Mrs. Emerson, the Multiple 26
Rose, the Philanthropist 28
Mrs. Woodruff, the Accused 30
Sally, the Victim 32
Sandra, the Writer 34
Stephanie, the Realist 36
Ceres, the Baker 38
Helen, the Daughter 40
Sharon, the Painter 42
Kali-Ya, the Warrior 44
Bes, the Child 46
Emily, the Mourner 48
Bridget, the Explorer 50
Nora, the Pedestrian 53
Alyson, the Grown-Up 55
Ethel, the Acupuncturist 56
Artie, the Single Girl 58
Constance, the Career Girl 60
Marcia, the Diver 62
Alexandra, the Music Lover 64
Barbara, the Swimmer 66
Kathryn, the Patient 68
Rosalind, the Repeater 70

Epilogue 73

Introduction

A few years ago, my friend Tammy Meneghini, who's a terrific professional actress, asked me to write a solo play for her. It had to have several distinct characters, since she would be performing it in conjunction with a specific movement method of acting which she was already using in her studio and which involved different energy sources in the performer's body. Her idea was to demonstrate this theory with my pieces; she would perform the show and offer workshops on this method.

We kicked around various possibilities and came up with female archetypes as my starting point: the virgin, the maiden, the lover, the crone, and so forth. It was a short leap to the concept of using goddesses from various myths as inspirations for contemporary takes. So I wrote about six monologues, which she loved and she began planning for performances and consequent workshops.

However, I found that I couldn't stop. New ideas kept popping into my head: every woman I saw or dealt with became a source of that magical "what if?" that writers always use. And soon I found that the ideas began to expand beyond goddesses. The women became more and more contemporary. They became more empowered, stronger, more varied. Some farcical ones that demanded to be written—like Doris, for instance—weren't about goddesses at all. I had a cacophony of stories.

And I soon realized that the monologues all had one thing in common: they were about women who had made or are making choices in their lives: some good, some bad; some lucky, some not; some funny, some tragic; some realistic, some fantastical. Hence my title: *Women of Choice.* And now there are thirty of them. Enough for a full evening of theater. Something like *For Colored Girls . . .* or *Talking With.*

Tammy chose some of them, which she now performs under the title *The Great Goddess Bazaar,* and which Jane Page directed. Information about Tammy and the show is on her website: goddesshere.com. But the monologues are available for others who might want to use them.

Here's the idea: any ensemble or production company or theater that would like to use these pieces can assemble any sort of evening they want by choosing and arranging the pieces to suit themselves. One production may be political, while another more humanistic. One may choose to focus on the bizarre and funny, while another may go for a more serious take, and a third might have a balance of the moods. One production may use three or four actors, each performing a variety, while another may have as many performers as they can fit. Any enterprising actress can gather an ensemble around her and go for it. Each performer can choose her own pieces if that works, while another may perform the choices made by the director of the producer.

In a sense, the *whole* evening is about women making choices.

You will also notice a prologue and an epilogue. Feel free to use them if they fit, or omit them if they don't. The play works equally well with or without a framing device. In other words, you can do whatever you want to make them work for you. I strongly suggest, however, that you start with Gail the Mother and end with either Kathryn the Patient or Rosalind the Repeater. These seem to be nice bookends.

There are only a few stipulations:

1. Nobody can perform a group of them alone. The rights to a one-person show belong exclusively to Miss Meneghini. However, a single actress can perform one monologue on her own, with proper permission and royalty payment.

2. No alterations, cuts, or emendations are allowed. The pieces are to be performed as written. I will be glad to work with any production to make changes that might be appropriate (such as word choices or references), but I reserve the author's right to make these decisions.

3. The standard copyright rules, restrictions and provisions for payment of royalties all apply. Please refer to the copyright page for these.

So here they are. Do what works for you. Make a choice.

###

Prologue

To my little one
As yet unformed, unborn,
Unrealized and waiting;

Welcome.
Come closer.

You have a great gift in store:
A lifetime of choices.

Good or ill, right or wrong—
They are all waiting for you.

Do not listen to those who tell you
You have no choices;
You may only choose this or that;
Your choice follows mine.
These are voices of fear or caution.

Ignore them, rise above them.

But would you see some of them that have come before?
Would you examine, consider, and explore?

Well then. Come

As we will end with a death,

Let us begin with a birth.

###

Theatre/opera references
Comedic
New mother
Recollection of an audition

3

GAIL, the Mother

My advice? Go with what you got. Case in point.

I go to this audition a wreck. Harry's kept Jim and me up all night. Harry's our ten-month-old, our first. He's at the stage where he's learning to manipulate the world through screams. You know the dilemma; is the little king crying because his di-dee is wet, or is he hungry, or is there a snake crawling up his crib. (We're theater-folk; with way too vivid imaginations.) Or is he screaming because he knows if he keeps it up long enough, I'll pick him up and sing "Vissi d'Arte?" He's becoming a spoiled brat, but at least he's a brat with taste.

Well, up until now we were "spoiling." He'd cry and one or both of us would go pick him up and sing Puccini. He especially liked stuff from *Boheme*. I wonder if that means anything? But now we'd decided to duke it out and let him cry himself to sleep. We'd put him in a dry diaper, given him plentiful suck, made sure there were no snakes, hummed a little "Humming Chorus"—and tiptoed out. And he started right up. Waa Waa Waa Waa. I mean, he was doing "Nessun Dorma" with a vengeance.

Which is why I'd been up that night. What to do? If we go in, he'll learn that when you call for help, you get warm fuzzy loving. If we let him cry himself to sleep, he'll learn the world is a hard, cruel place. We'd opted for hard and cruel. They don't call it "tough love" for nothing.

So back to the audition. It's for Gertrude at Colorado Shakes. If I got it, it would be this big step forward. I mean, I was doing okay for a while, on a nice, slow but steady uphill slog, with a little time off to get pregnant. I had worked a lot here and there on the in-genues—Celia, Hero, Adriana—but this was jumping into serious deep waters.

So I was nervous. A major theater, a chance to do a role with some meat on it and I'm thinking I'm probably way too young to be Hamlet's mother. Unless Gertrude was married at ten, but maybe they did that in Denmark in those days. So, okay, I could go with that. Maybe I could bill and coo a little. Yes. No. Funny. Sad. I'm a wreck. The only thing going for me is that, for some reason, God chose to give me a very good hair day.

So I'm sitting in the hallway, running lines in my head:
"O Hamlet, speak no more;
Thou turn'st mine eyes into my very soul;
And there I see such black and grained spots
As will not leave their tinct."

And Jim calls my cell phone. "The baby's got a fever. Ninety-nine point seven; maybe you should come home?" "I'm next, honey; can you wait half an hour and take it again?" "Is this what it's gonna be like? I thought you said you weren't gonna let the career screw up the baby." "Jim, we're talking 99.7, it's not the last stages of consumption here!" "Okay, if that's your call. Go ahead; break a leg."

Fine. Now my concentration's gone. I obsess about motherhood. *Hamlet, speak no more,* maybe he's right, I'm being selfish. *Thou turn'st mine eyes into my very soul;* after all, the kid IS going through rough times; *And there I see such black and grained spots.* Maybe this is a big mistake. And then I'm called. Totally unresolved.

So now I'm there with the stage manager, reading the closet scene and something weird happens. I understood the scene. No, I don't mean I knew what the words meant, even "tinct." I suddenly realized that, for good or for bad, I was what Gertrude was. I was a mother too. Just like her. I mean, Gertrude probably had a wet nurse, and a dozen nannies at her beck and call. She never had to sit up all night listening to baby Hamlet scream his heart out, but she must have watched him grow. She must have been there for his first steps, seen him win his first footrace. She must have watched him watching Ophelia and had some thoughts about that. He must have even been somewhere in the back of her head while she was sporting through incestuous sheets. So we were, somehow, connected by archetype. Could I use that?

I mean, I had resisted going up for real mother roles because I thought I was wrong for them, or because I had always thought they were somehow lesser. But suddenly I had a new mantra, because little Harry popped into my head. Harry having his first disappointment last night, slowly learning that the world can break your heart. Harry as Hamlet. Hamlet as Harry. And somewhere inside me, I felt the touch of his skin, the smell of his breath, the sound of his voice. I felt transformed. Suddenly I knew everything about the world, and all I had to do was let myself open up to it.

Now I know some actresses will scoff and say, "Hey, it's your basic Stanislavski, Magic If, emotional recall," blah blah blah. But it was more than that. It was some cosmic stirring of a maternal power that only women understand.

I soared through the audition. Walking out, I knew I'd get the part. I was frighteningly psychic. I knew that Henry's temperature was only a slight nothing. I knew that he would sleep through the night from now on. I knew that he would play basketball in high school and would choose medical school over theater. I knew that Jim and I would have more kids. I knew that I would get great notices as Gertrude and that my career would climb, that I would grow old and would have grandchildren and that I would die before Jim but that I would cross the finish line on my own two feet.

I said, "Thank you," to the director when he said, "Very good. We'll be in touch." And I walked home, under a clear and sunny sky.

And I laughed all the way there.

###

Emotional
Heavy American accent
Twist at the end
Damaged husband disrupts their family life 5

MARY, the Widow

Forgive me, Father, for I have sinned. It's been a long time since my last confession. Is that a sin too? I don't even know if it matters now, compared to what I done.

It's Nick, you see, my husband. When he came back from the war, he was different. At first, only *I* could tell. There were small things nobody would notice but me, like—like how he kissed me wasn't the same. Not at first; at first it was like our honeymoon all over again—well, except for the boys—but after a while it was different. I mean, he would go through the motions but he didn't really mean it.

I kept asking him if there was something wrong, was it the war? He didn't want to talk about it. So, I figured it was an adjustment thing, maybe he couldn't open up because he had to get used to being safe. But then it got worse.

He started acting weird to other people. Like with Harold. Me and him and Betsy and Harold, we used to bowl; once a month we'd throw a couple of lines and drink beer and laugh. But that went wrong too. He wasn't throwing like he used to. He used to make Back Rows or Big Fours and whatever like they was nothing but no more. One time, Harold was kidding and he said something like "They musta fucked with your eyes over there!" and Nick, he got pissed. "Mind your own fucking business," and when Harold started going "Hey, hey, man, I'm joking," and like that, Nick hauled off and knocked him over the return and near broke his arm. I mean, him and Harold, they made up right away, but we never went bowling again.

And he started having trouble at work. He went back to his old job at the Ford place on Ava Road; he was a genius with motors, he could figure out the problem and have it fixed before you could blink. But he started making mistakes. I know zero about cars, but he would come home depressed and he would say things like he couldn't figure this out or he fucked up with that or it was so loud in the bays you couldn't hear yourself think. I said maybe because while he was gone, they changed things so much and he called me a dumb bitch and I should mind my own business. I said I was only trying to help, and he shouts how he could take care of himself and like that and the boys would wake up and start crying and it was terrible

I figured maybe it was that thing soldiers get when they come back. Post-trauma disease or whatever. I told him he oughta get some help. So he went to this clinic. But when he came home, he said they were a bunch of assholes who all they wanted him to do was talk about it when all he wanted to do was forget about it, so he didn't go back again.

Then started the nightmares. Muttering and grunting, the only words I could make out was "too late." He'd keep saying that: "too late." I asked him to tell me; he said he didn't want to talk about it, nothing to worry about. Until the day he went after the boys. It was after church on Sunday; he stopped going to church with us, too; he used to love it, though; he even sang in the choir. But he gave that up. So here he is: him and the boys out playing catch, and he says: "Let's play a different game, let's play capture the flag. I'm the good guy, you're the bad guys, and one of you grabs the flag and tries to get past the home base line before I tackle you." I heard him from the kitchen window while I was making supper. Well, he puts this handkerchief in the middle of the yard, and he goes to one side and the boys go to the other and he gives this signal and they start running. Franky grabs the flag first—I figured he let him, right? He's a good dad—and they started back to their home base. But then something happens, he would never talk about it afterwards, but he suddenly starts screaming and yelling at 'em, calling 'em weird bastards, gooks, fucking pieces of shit and he runs after 'em, and he tackles Franky and throws him on the ground and starts . . . he starts hitting him, not like in play but like he's really trying to kill him. Franky starts yelling, and Mickey starts pulling at him and shouting, and Nick is smashing at Franky, and I ran out there with the rolling pin in my hand and I start pummeling Nick on his shoulder trying to make him stop.

Finally he does. The kids are crying, I'm feeling sick, Nick goes up in our room and shuts himself in and don't come down for supper and it was hell like that for a couple of days. He finally goes into the boys' room one night, and somehow he got them to understand how he was sorry, they were good boys, and like that. They seemed okay, except after that, every time he went to hug one of 'em, you could see 'em shiver a little.

So here's what I don't know about, Father, okay? How he died. You know the story: He tiptoed out of bed, went into the garage, closed all the doors, and turned on the engine and before you could say "boo," he was gone. It was in the obits, everybody was sad, I got lots of flowers and casseroles, and it was hell. But . . . the part that hurts isn't that. The part that hurts is this.

Our bedroom is over the garage. I heard him getting out of bed. I heard him going downstairs. I heard the door into the garage open. I heard him turning on the motor. I smelled the gasoline. I knew what he was doing. But I didn't go down and stop him. All I hadda do was go down there and press the little red button that opens the garage door. It woulda been that simple, and he'd be here today.

But I didn't. I didn't do nothing, Father. I figured how could we go on like that. I figured the boys would suffer. I figured it's what he woulda wanted. I don't know what I figured anymore.

So did I do right, Father? Did I do wrong? Like, is this gonna take a hundred Hail Marys or something?

###

Job Interview
Married to the wrong man and was stuck but stayed faithful.
Finally freed after his death
Older woman

7

NANCY, the Wife

I married Andrew for all the wrong reasons and spent the rest of my life paying for it. But I was a good wife and mother. I never cheated. I deserve credit for that much at least.

You have to understand that my sister Janet and I were brought up in competition. I was older but she was favored: the athlete, the smart one, and try as hard as I could, I couldn't beat her. But I evened the score when I married first. Andrew came along and he seemed nice.

And so we married. But I hadn't beaten my sister at all. What I did was seal myself into second place for the rest of my life. Because Andrew turned out to be Peter Pan, one of those sad men who never grow up. He didn't want a wife: he wanted a Wendy. For instance, his job: He worked as a shoe salesman all of his life, and always in the same store. He never moved: once they wanted to make him a manager, he refused. It was too much responsibility, he said.

Or the housekeeping. Once I went away for a weekend for a golf tournament out of town. When I got back on Sunday night, the place was a war zone. Take-out Chinese-food boxes all over, dishes piled in the sink, the bed unmade—not that I expected him to be the wife, but when I asked him why he didn't at least wash the dishes, he looked confused and hurt. "There's not that many," he said. "And besides, I don't know where you keep the soap."

We had three boys. He was disappointed; he wanted at least one daughter. And of course he left all the parenting up to me. When John broke his leg, I rushed him to the hospital because Andrew went hysterical. When Jeremy was mobbed, beaten—fag-bashed is the term—I sat with him all night while he trembled and I went to the school and I organized the P-FLAG club because Andrew couldn't accept the fact that one of his sons was, as he called it, "spoiled." And as for Dennis, Andrew simply paid him no attention at all, because Dennis was an accident. We'd agreed to stop at two so he thought I'd done it on purpose just to spite him.

But the truth is, in his heart, Andrew was jealous of them all, because every ounce of attention I gave them, I took away from him. So I became a mother to four boys. Cook, nurse, financial advisor: I handed out their allowances—even Andrew: he'd turn his paycheck over to me and I gave him spending money. I paid the bills, I did our taxes, I watched our investments. The boys all went to good schools and got good jobs. We had a very nice nest egg for retirement. I did it all and I never complained and I never cheated. I deserve credit for that at least.

And then when Robert came along, the manager where I played golf, I saw that as a test. I wasn't looking for it, you have to understand that. But he was sweet and never pushed. We had dinner when we could—I told Andrew it was a book club meeting. We'd meet for a movie or a drink, but it didn't go anywhere beyond a quick hug. It was a test. And I passed it. I never cheated. I never complained to the boys, I never set them against their father, I never missed a meal, the house was spotless, the bank account balanced every month, I slept with Andrew whenever he asked; I gave up golf and never saw Robert again. I deserve full credit, for that much at least.

And then of course when Andrew had his heart attack, that was another test. The boys were all gone by then. By then I'd realized that they had been the marriage. All the noise, the connecting, all the giving and getting of love—I had gradually given everything to my boys and saved nothing for myself. For a time, behind Andrew's back, I began reading the want-ads, practicing my typing skills. I read self-help books about divorce and mid-life crisis and I made myself ready.

But then, of course, came the heart attack. Fifteen seconds and there was a noose around my neck. I sometimes wonder if Andrew did it on purpose. But I sat by his bed day and night. I never went home. I had married him for sickness and health and all that and I wasn't going to bail so I sat there and slept in the chair, the boys bought me clean clothes and I used the shower in his room. One time I heard one of the nurses saying to another: "She must love that cross so much she just carries it around all the time." I ignored it. They couldn't know what I was doing; they couldn't appreciate how . . . proud . . . how . . . satisfied . . . it made me feel. I knew Janice wouldn't have ever done what I did.

And then it was finally over. He was dead and I was free. Yes, that's the word; exactly how I felt. And so I applied for this job. As you can see on my application, I type 125 words a minute, I do double-entry bookkeeping. I bought myself a computer and can use half a dozen software programs.

Test me. Give me a trial. You'll find I'm a very solid, dedicated person. I'm a good worker. I stick to a job no matter what. When I start something, I finish it. I never complain and I never cheat. I deserve credit for that much at least.

Full credit.

###

ARIADNE, the Spinner

Can we meet on this next Thursday at 8:17? No, I can't do 9:30, I have Faculty Senate, I'm on the procedures committee and we're voting on bagels or donuts for the spring picnic. Last year the donuts were stale yet again and I brought up bagels and before you knew it, I was chairing the subcommittee. We have to be out by 11:00, so we could meet at 11:06. No, wait; that won't work for me; I'm helping Virginia on her grant application. She wants to dig for ancient scrolls in Cleveland. Her theory is that the lost tribes of Israel settled by Lake Erie somewhere during the Ching-Ching Dynasty but she's having trouble coming up with a rationale so I'm making one up for her. Won't it be exciting when we get it?

So that means next week. I could do Monday at 5:18 to 6:03, we'll be on our supper break at the President's dinner committee. We're trying to decide on green or beige. I'm opting for beige because as soon as I think of green, I think "Save the Whales" and it reminds me I still haven't written my foreword to Hester's book on Melville and besides, beige coordinates with anything you want to wear, and NO-body looks good in green.

There's Tuesday—I'm at the dentist 3:19 to 5:02, I should be back by 5:30. No, wait. I'm meeting Charles Upson on his term paper. The poor boy just doesn't get it. We've been using MLA for years, but he always goes Chicago and simply nobody uses Chicago anymore. I mean a footnote is *not* a citation, for heaven's sake. Even worse: I found seven misplaced commas in his introduction alone. So we could talk around nine? No problem; I'm up to at least midnight, and that's on a good day.

Wednesday is my work-at-home day. I have three papers to pound out for ASFLAGA by the end of the week. ASFLAGA? The American Society For Liberal Arts General Academics. You mean you haven't joined? Don't you *care* about your career? I chair the hotel committee. They want to use the Hilton again, but the last time we were there, the maids forgot to turn down the beds, at least in my room, so who knows what else they're cheating us on? It'll be the Executive Manor, or I'm resigning. Why do I need three papers? Well, one is "The Pre-Raphaelite Syndrome, Fact or Myth?" Two is "A Geopolitical Reassessment of Third-World Revisionist Trade Practices," and three—well nobody has ever defined comedic tragedy in Middle-Earth, at least not to *my* satisfaction. Plus I'm responding to a panel on plagiarism in the freshman biology class. It's just getting out of hand. Last year alone, there were twenty-five reports from land grant universities on students copying their dissection reports from the Internet. I mean, first frogs and then anarchy; look how we elect our presidents!

But I'm free for lunch on Thursday after my class—but wait: I can't make this out. Oh; lunch with Gloria. I have to keep my work-study assistants happy, you know: my research into amphibious symbolism in the works of Samuel Beckett alone takes up seven hours a week; where would *I* find the time?

Friday, can you make any time between 3:07 and 7:03? We could have supper. Oh, your wife; of course she wants to see you once in a while. Not everybody is as understanding as Sebastian was. My late husband, he died before you started here. No, we were too busy for kids. How's two weeks from Monday?

Oh, no, I couldn't possibly squeeze you in next week. I'm on the homecoming special events committee, there's something every day. Decorating the stadium; supper for the football team—they look forward to my pork roast, I can't disappoint them—and who do you think writes the coach's welcoming address at the Starlight Dinner and chooses the menu? It would take me a whole day to list my chores for the week. Say "No?" Impossible: If you want something done right, you have to do it yourself.

So two weeks from Monday—no, better make it Tuesday—I'll need a day to recuperate. The Chancellor's Ball *alone* is hell in a basket, especially since I have to hire the band and select their music AND deal with the caterer who NEVER brings enough wine selections. I give them a list every year, but do they read it? Too much cabernet, never enough Riesling.

So we're looking two weeks from Tuesday. Tuesday's my rough teaching day; I have four classes in a row; but there's that Wednesday. . . . No, wait. That's the one day a month I volunteer at the Recycle Center. I help them sort out colored newspaper from plain. You'd be appalled at how many people can't tell the difference between them; what really screws them up is the Sunday funnies. I swear, it's a miracle we have ANY recycled toilet paper at all. But wait, wait: I could switch. I could do my recycling on third Thursdays if I could get Sonja McGuffin to switch Kindergarten Traffic Cop Day with me. So are you free the fourth Thursday after that? I'm looking at the 18th of March.

No, the rest of March is totally gone. We're hosting the East-Eurasian Women's Frisbee team again and I'm putting them all up at my house. I do this every other year. It's my one time to hang with the gals, if you know what I mean.

That gets me into April, when I teach my nighttime "Do Your Taxes" Class at the Senior Center. Wait . . . wait; here we go! Monday, April 31st at 7:46 AM. I have a whole two hours sitting just waiting for something do to. It'll be perfect.

I know, how do I do it? It's all in the notebook. And yet . . . somehow . . . I keep having the feeling there's something I'm missing. Something that I need to do today. Oh, yes, yes, of course: It's the anniversary of Sebastian's death. I have to go out to the cemetery and plant a rose. He loved roses.

How could I have forgotten that?

###

DORIS, the Star

OFFSTAGE ANNOUNCER:
Ladies and Gentlemen. And now . . . that great woman of the musical theater, Broadway's darling; a legend in her own time; live and in person: An Evening with Doris Fazzoli!!!!

(Sounds of applause. DORIS appears. SHE sings full-out belting *a capella*. NOTE TO ACTRESS: Some of the lyrics here are parodies from real songs, use the melodies if possible. For others, make up your own melody as you like. All songs except the last should be sung a-la-belter.)

DORIS:
(made up tune)
HELLO, EVERYBODY, HELLO;
HELLO, EVERYBODY, HELLO;
I'M SO GLAD I'M HERE TODAY,
ALL I CAN DO IS SMILE AND SAY,
HELLO, EVERYBODY, HELLO.
HELLOOOOOOOOOOOOOOO!

Hello! How is everybody? I am so thrilled to be here, I can't tell you. Although, at my age, I'm just glad to be anywhere. I just had my hip replaced, my shoulder is new, my knees are new, my boobs are fake, my teeth go into a glass at night. I need an instruction manual to put myself together every morning!
(fake laugh)
The only thing real about me is my heart, full of love for all you wonderful fans and the voice God blessed me with. After all,
(made up tune)
YOU GOTTA LIVE TILL YOU DIE;
NO MATTER WHERE, NO MATTER WHY;
YOU GOTTA LIVE LIVE LIVE TILL YOU DIE!

But you didn't come here to listen to me preach at you. You wanta hear stories, you wanta find out the answer to the age-old question: What is Doris Fazzoli really like? Well, I have here the question cards you filled out when you came in. I'll pick some out and give you an answer. And if the answer makes me feel like singing, I'll do that too. Let's have some fun.

"How did you get started?" Ah, good.

LET'S START AT THE VERY BEGINNING,
A HELLUVA PLACE TO START.

It was in high school. Picture this: A tall, gawky thing with glasses the size of owl-eyes. I had such bad acne it was like "connect-the-dots" on my face. I hadda do something. They were doing the spring musical, it was *Oklahoma*—isn't that a wonderful show, ladies and gentlemen? I once met Richard Rodgers, he became a dear friend; he asked me to do

The Sound of Music, did you know that? I told him, I said, "Dick, honey, you're out of your freaking mind. Do you think anybody in their wildest dreams could believe ME in a nunnery? A bordello in Cleveland, maybe, but don't push your luck!" Anyhow, there I was, the biggest geek in town and I thought "You ain't got nothing to lose, honey, just do it." And somebody up there must've taken pity on me because they gave me the part of I Do Annie. You know, she gets to sing that wonderful song:

I'M JUST A GIRL WHO WON'T SAY NO.
NO NO NO NO NO NO NO!

And they loved me. So I said to myself, "Doris, honey, I think you're on to something! If you can make 'em laugh, maybe you'll find love that way." But I'm getting choked up. Let's see what else we have here:

"I want to be a musical star just like you. What was your big break?"
I'd say it was when I was walking along Christopher Street down in the village and there was a little restaurant there, and I was hungry. Seemed I spent most of that first week in New York being hungry. To this day I can't walk through Times Square without buying bagels. You can tell, can't you? But hey, the more there is of me, the more there is to love, and you know what I'm talking about, honey.

(made up tune)
I'M THE LAST OF THE BIG TIME MOMMAS.
YOU SHOULD SEE ME IN MY PAJAMAS.
WHEN I WALK, THE BUILDINGS QUIVER,
BUT WHEN YOU WANT ME, HONEY, CAN I DELIVER!
THE LAST OF THE BIG TIME MOMMAS, THAT'S ME.

So I walked in and went up to the owner. "Listen, Mister. I need a meal. I don't have any money, but if you give me a hamburger, I'll sing for your customers." Well, he went and said yes, and there I was.

SOMEWHERE BEYOND THE RAINBOW
IN THE SKY . . .
YOU AND I . . .
DO OR DIE.

Well, would you believe, right there having lunch that day was a man who wrote a few songs in his day, Mr. Irving Berlin. I count him not only my benefactor, but a dear, dear friend. He came up to me and gave me his card and next thing I know I'm in the chorus of a show and before you can say "Hey Momma, hit me, I'm dreamin'," I'm playing the lead in *Annie Where's Your Gun?* in a bus and truck in Pittsburgh. So the point, honey, is just send your heart out into the universe and sooner than later the universe will pay you back. Hell, if I can do it, so can you.

Next question: "What do you think of the critics and why do you think they hate you so much?"

You know, I've often asked myself the same thing. I think it's jealousy. It takes guts to do what I do. I go out there every night I can, and I give a hundred and ten per cent of what I got. And I think most critics are jealous of that, because they either ain't got the talent, or worse: ain't got the guts. So when they see somebody like me, who's been doing this a hundred and fifty years and still won't quit, why they just see their own fears and regrets and failures, and they just like to take it out on the defenseless. They're just cowards and shirkers and wallflowers at the dance and there ought to be a special circle in hell for them.

But other than that, I don't really pay them much attention.

Time for just a few more. "Is there any truth to the rumors about you and—" No.

"What's the real story behind your long-running feud with Liza?" Liza who?

"What is the one thing you want to be remembered as?" Ahh, a good question. I've often thought of that, alone by myself. "What's it all about, Doris? Why?" It's like I said earlier; I'm a vessel, ladies and gentlemen. I think of myself as a force, an energy, a spirit, if you will. Something eternal and useful, that happens for this time to live in this body. Sometimes it's in another body, like Abraham Lincoln or Moses or Helen Keller or Mahatma Gandhi or Shirley Temple or Babe Ruth or Jesus or Lassie—but whatever form it takes, it's here for one purpose only. To make us better human beings. And if one of my songs can do that, why, darling, that's the best memorial a singer could have.

Last one: "Would you sing your favorite song?"

(Very simply and beautifully, SHE sings: *)

AMAZING GRACE, HOW SWEET THE SOUND
THAT SAVED A WRETCH LIKE ME;
I ONCE WAS LOST, BUT NOW AM FOUND,
WAS BLIND, BUT NOW I SEE.

(* NOTE: Feel free to substitute any similar song: something plaintive, beautiful, simple.)

MICHELLE, the Soldier

So, okay, listen up. This is off the record, because they don't like to admit there's a problem. The bottom line is this: you don't ever want to go pee alone, especially at night. Somebody is waiting for you, you can bet your life. In fact, that's just what you're doing. Because, ladies, once you've been raped, you're raped for life.

Of course it sucks. You join the military because you wanta do something good or whatever. There's enemy out there, we're all on the same team; so you shouldn't have to worry about your own guys, right?

But come on, ladies. Remember: in the first place, they're guys. Guys always think with their junk. In the second place, they're soldiers; trained to be dogs at war. If they ain't thinking with their wands, they're thinking with their rifles, which to some guys is the same thing. Power is currency here. And in the third place, most of 'em are scum to begin with. This army's hurting so bad for grunt, they take anybody who can walk and breathe at the same time. Used to matter if you had a record, like if you were a hophead, a dealer, or some juvie working off his years. Or else they're poor shits that got redeployed and so who are they pissed at? Who do they take it out on? You know what I'm talking about.

The other part of the problem is that there's more of us around, more women doing ground combat than in World Wars I and II put together. And what makes it worse is that everything that goes down around here is ground combat. Used to be there were lines. You were on the front line or behind the line. Now every place you go, walk or drive, could be the front line; and that makes you tense all the time. That's why there's so much booze and pot and sex. This place is loaded with sex. Sex tension. Sex talk. Sex think. And all that, ladies—all that is only one zipper away from sex do.

This is where peeing comes into the picture. You heard about Millie Thompson, who died in her cot from dehydration because she wouldn't drink anything after three o'clock. Out here in the desert you almost gotta be crazy to go dry like that. Right, but when you think what she was facing by having to go pee after dark, you gotta wonder where the biggest danger was. She chose to be stupid. I'm here to tell you how to be smart.

There are three things to keep in mind. I called them the "Upa Rules"; that's the name of this group I started: Upa. U-P-A. Which stands for three danger signs. When any one of these three are in place, you're at high risk. So that's U for Unarmed. P for Private. And A for Alone. Any time you're either unarmed, or in any kind of private place, or alone, you're asking for trouble.

I speak from experience, ladies. I was on a medical detail, helping evacuate Iraqis from this bombsite. We were using some old trucks, and me and this guy, a guy I'd worked side by side with for like three weeks and I thought I knew him. But then on the way back, the truck was empty, he suddenly pulls off the road and stops the car. And he turns to me and he starts in: "Do you know how fucking sexy you are? I had this big hard-on for you since I saw you." I told him to quit it, and get back on the road; I mean, there were wounded and dying waiting and this prick gets horny with me. I tell him to stop, I'm gonna report him, I don't even remember what I said but I fought back hard as I could, and suddenly he's on me, and I'm flat on my back across the seat, I don't even remember how I got that way, and he's pushing into me moaning over and over again. And when he's done, he grunts at me: "You talk and you're dead meat, get it?"

You see? Upa. I was Unarmed. But ever since then, I carry a knife with me. And I was in a Private place. You wouldn't have thought the front seat of a Ford qualified as private, but there it was. A latrine is private, a porta-john is private, the supply closet in your building is private. And I was alone, and of course by that I mean I was the only woman there because the truth is: you could be in a room with two dozen guys and if you're the only woman there, you're alone like if you were on the moon.

What did I do about it? Everything I was supposed to. I followed all the channels. I reported it to my CO. He did nothing. I contacted SAPR like they told us to and got a ton of paper work tossed at me. I got on the Web and found one crisis center after another, a dozen phone numbers. And I got zip in return. Either nobody believed me, or they thought, like they always do, that I was quote "asking for it" or—worse—that I was a troublemaker making waves. I was this big national traitor for taking up the army's time on useless crap when there was a war going on. You understand? I was still Upa: Unprotected, Private and Alone.

Well, let me cut to the chase before they find out we're here. That guy, that shit doctor who raped me: they found him on the road the other day: he must've been drunk or stoned and didn't see the truck coming at him. That's what they say. It's an easy answer, makes sense, and nobody has to do anything about it. Just like they hushed-up and lied about my rape, they covered up the accident and let it ride. And then I started this group. Upa, that nobody knows about except us. That O'Hara belongs to, who got attacked in a supply closet. And some soldier died from food poisoning. That Forsythe belongs to, who got ganged in a kitchen. And then these three grunts were taken out by accidental friendly fire. That each of these women sitting in the front row belongs to, all of them got stories that won't get in the papers.

So here's the bottom line, ladies. Never be Unprotected. Never be Private. And never be Alone. And if something does happen, you don't bother with channels, you hear me? You come see us. Any one of us. We'll take care of it. We'll take care of it good.

###

22

APHRODITE, the Street Lady

So, George, the pig, he says, "I want my spaghetti in short pieces; shlurping up noodles is a fucking hassle." I says, "That's how they're made, what the hell do you want me to do?" "Cut 'em up," he says. "You're out of your mind, I'm supposed to stand there with a scissors and cut up each piece?" So then he rips the box open, he pours all the noodles out, he grabs both ends in one bunch breaks 'em in half. "See?" he says. "You have to go to school to be that stupid?" Well, I don't take that from nobody. I pack up a pillowcase with stuff and walk out. He's probably still sitting there, waiting for the fucking noodles to boil. Or maybe he's starved to death. He never had the brains of a pissant; he couldn't even boil water unless I was standing there showing him how.

You're better off alone. The street is better.

Richard and me, we're in the zoo one time by the elephant cage. And he says, "You know, elephants are a lot like people. Better. Like, when an elephant dies, all the other elephants, they come around in a circle, and they give it some attention. It don't die alone. Now people don't do that. People aren't half so good as elephants." "You're nuts," I says; "Elephants. What the fuck do they know?"

Richard got killed in the war. It hurt like hell. The street is better.

I wish the Pope would come. Last time the Pope came, they took us all into the shelter for a week. "For charity," they said. Right. The second his plane took off, they put us back on the street. God forbid we should make the city look dirty.

Ira used to go to confession every day. Before he came home, he stopped at St. Bart's to get on his knees. "It makes me close to God," he says. "You could get close to me once in a while; you got some pussy on the side?" "You're a pig," he says; "You don't shave no more. It's like a fucking jungle down there." What kind of thing is that to say to your wife? I walked out the next week. I cleaned out the checking account, he didn't even know it.

Elephants. What the fuck do they know?

Stanley, the idiot, I told him, "Get some kid to shovel that; you're old and fat." I saw him drop. And then his kid, the one he had with Marion, comes along and blames me. She's pissed because I got all the insurance money. What good was it? Once I paid the shyster funeral home and the double-shyster lawyer and the fucking triple-shyster medical fucking bills, I had to sell the house anyhow.

When the Pope was here, that was alright. He shoulda stayed a month. I wonder if they're gonna have beef stew at the shelter tonight. They always undercook it, but it's hot.

Warren, now he could cook. Easter was his specialty. He could glaze a ham so you could see your face in it. Asparagus, crunchy with butter, like biting into a real expensive chocolate chip cookie. Parker House rolls, soft as a pillow. And coffee. You could get drunk on his coffee. Too bad he couldn't keep his dick in his pants. Especially with that whore from the factory. Like he didn't think I'd ever find out?

I must be an asshole magnet; something you're born with. I went to confession. "What's wrong with me, Father?" I says. "Every guy, every single one. Maybe I should turn lesbo." He coughs. "God isn't a dating service," he says. "There are websites for that purpose. Now, what is your sin?" "My fucking sin, Father," I says, "Is coming here in the first place."

My sister, now there's a holy person for you. She's been with Sammy 30 years now. I can't stand him, he's got wandering hands, but she puts up with it. She knows what hand feeds her, gives her that condo in Texas, puts 500-dollar dresses on her skanky back. "Don't that make you feel like a whore?" I says. "Don't come back 'til you apologize." Yeah, fuck that: pigs will fly first. He probably gave her the clap again, like he did with that Mexican tramp from the post office. Like it's my fault? Like if I hadn't've told her somebody else wouldn't't've?

Men are pigs.

Henry was decent. I got lucky with Henry. He gave me respect. I mean, who opens door for women any more? Who takes your arm crossing Main and Walnut? Who remembers birthdays? The time I was sick. He read to me. "Alice was beginning to get very tired sitting by herself on the bank." Afterwards I read it again myself. I read that book so many times since I almost memorized it. It was that quack at the clinic. I shoulda been more careful. Maybe I even shoulda had the baby. Maybe I shoulda told Henry, but as long as he thought it was bleeding ulcers, everybody was happy. He didn't have to know. It would've made him miserable. Maybe I shoulda stayed with him. No. Every time I looked at his face, his eyes looking at me with all that. Trust. No. This is better. I woulda made a lousy mother. I don't have what it takes. Patience, you know what I mean? I don't think I got enough patience.

The street is better.

I mean, elephants: what the fuck do they know.

###

MINERVA, the Teacher

Theresa? You feeling better, bless your heart? That's good; you need the rest. Tonight? Went fine. Lord knows you cover for me when I need you. You know I don't like doing first-timers as a rule. They take forever and they don't tip. But this turned out very different. This changed my life. Pour some bourbon in your chicken soup and put your feet up.

Here's the picture. I'm at the Walgreen's in the mall at 8:30 like we arranged, wearing this red beret-thing and carrying some Stephen King. Why this kid couldn't just give me his address and pay me cab fare, I don't know. Hell, it's just getting laid; what's the big adventure?

So he shows up in this cowboy hat and I'm thinking this piece of candy ain't 18 if he's a day, and it is time to split. But on the other hand, he is gorgeous. Tall, blue eyes, shoulders out to next Wednesday, and a candy-ass butt you just *have* to touch! And he goes "Hot night," And I go "Warm enough for December," and he goes "You Miss Kitty?" and, because this is getting stupid, I go "Sweetheart, as long as we're asking questions, just how freaking old are you?" He smiles at me: "I'm 22." And I'm thinking twice, but those baby blues, you know what I'm saying, and I start laughing and he starts laughing and bam! We're in his Honda Civic ripping 75 with the top down and the wind flapping his long yellow hair like a flag.

And, of course, he's yakking away so I knew it's his first time. His folks are out of town, he and his buddies decided tonight is cherry picking time." And I go, "So you're all of you, like amateur night or something?" And he goes, "Except me. I been screwing Angela for months now; I done it in five different positions and once on the kitchen table and I even got her off one time too." I know it's bullshit, but I'm thinking, there oughta be a law against anybody *ever* being that young!

So we get into his apartment and there are three other guys waiting for us. One's a big hulking guy who says his name is Mike; he's got this bald head which I hate, but at the same time you can see he's trying like hell to grow a beard. There's this tall thin stick of wood who says his name is Jason, he just nods and giggles and picks at his nose. And there's a shorter, little guy, who's got a face like one of them angels you see on Christmas cards. He tells me his name is Anthony, but I can tell that out of all four of them, he's the only one lying.

Well, we have a drink—me just the Coke I brought myself—and he shows me the bedroom. And so it goes. You been there too. One by one, in they come, four little cubbies looking to become big bears. And I'm remembering what you told me once about the little ones, how each is exactly the same but at the same time they're all different. So in they come one at a time, each with the same kind of grin on his face, dressed in his tighty whites, and holding out his hand when he comes in, showing me the condom like it was some holy offering. So I show him how to put the little glove on, lay back, and wait for him to climb on board.

And now it gets really interesting. I start imagining what these guys are gonna be like in—oh, say, a couple dozen years. You can tell a lot about a guy from the way he screws, especially when he's 17 years old.

So Gregory is first. He kneels on top of me showing off his wand and asking me if I ever saw one that big and I'm in for the treat of my life cuz he knows how to make a woman scream in pleasure and he starts tickling my tits and my belly and I'm thinking this guy's been around way too much porn. I invite him to step right in, he does, and bam, bam, bam—we're done. This, I'm thinking, this guy is gonna be a lawyer.

Next is Mike, the bruiser. He takes his whitey off under the covers with me and starts asking me questions. "How did I get started doing this?" "What's the best position for a woman?" I finally have to remind him that we got people waiting. So he climbs in, but he keeps on talking. "How's that?" "Where's that magic spot?" And then all of a sudden he's very quiet, then I hear a soft little "oop" and he slides out. This, I'm thinking, this guy is gonna be a priest.

The tall stick of wood says nothing at all. At least 'til he's inside. And then he turns weird on me. He pounds at me, hard, like some pile driver. Then he starts grunting—not words, but caveman sounds and I can't decide if he's getting off or having a heart attack. And he takes for freaking-ever until he pops with, I swear to God, he goes "Hallelujah, Brooklyn!" Then he climbs out and shakes my hand and I'm thinking this guy is gonna run for governor.

And then in comes Anthony, or whatever his real name is. And I didn't even need two seconds to figure him out. He stands there at the side of the bed looking at me like a puppy who just had an accident. I look up at him. "You don't really wanta do this, do you?" He shakes his head. "We'll just say you did, how's that?" He nods. I tell him to sit down and tell me about himself, and he looks at me and he lays his head on my breast and cries. So I let him lay there and I rub his shoulders, and I tell him the story about my cousin Jeffrey and the chicken. And before long we're laughing and I'm thinking, this one—well I don't have to tell you. I just hope he gets through high school in one piece.

So, there they were. I finish the night off; I wash each one of them a little, I pick up the envelope with my name on it—and for some reason I don't open it and count it like I usually do—I get Gregory to call me a cab, and I'm gone. And here's the weird part. So now I'm riding home wondering what the hell just happened to me. Because something is changed; something inside me is new and different.

And I decide—you ready?—I'm changing careers. I'm gonna sign up with the city schools and become a sub. Yeah, a sub, I mean it.

I'm thinking I got a lot to teach young kids nowadays.

###

MRS. EMERSON, the Multiple

You're new; what happened to Dr. Swadley? . . . Oh. When? . . . All those cigarettes, huh? Serves her right. She'd come in here, reeking of smoke and the one time I told her she oughta quit, she said she was the doctor, I was the patient, and mind my own business. I bet now she's sorry she didn't listen to me.

Okay. Down to business, huh? . . . Why did I take all those pills? Because of my voices, it should all be there in the record. . . . How can it be all scribbles: I talked and she wrote everything down.

Okay. From the beginning.

The first was right after Joe walked out. Maybe they knew I was lonely so they started talking to me. I was in the Walmart, by the eggs, trying to decide medium or large—I was on this tight budget now, especially with two kids. And she said, "The bigger is the better value. You get a few grams more protein." . . . She? The voice of the Lady, who do you *think* I'm talking about! . . . Odd? Yeah, well, of course it seemed odd. But she sounded friendly. You can't have enough friends in this world.

Then the others started. Hey, you don't happen to have a cigarette on you, do you? They relax me; talking about my voices makes me nervous with other people, they think I'm crazy. . . . Okay. Right, take a lesson from Dr. Swadley, I know. So, okay. The others.

There was the Lady; she helped me around the house. Like shopping, or cooking, she always knew exactly when the rice was done. The Secretary; she reminded me of things I had to do. Take the kids to the day care. Go pick them up. Remember to buy rice. The Nazi; she was always scolding me for something I was doing wrong. Like for instance when I stole those panties from Walmart. But who is she to talk; she doesn't have to pay the bills. . . . Okay, okay. Then there was the Little Girl; she'd sing; sometimes all you need is to hear some sweet little girl singing. And, oh, yes. there was the Knight. He was . . . well, he was with me in bed when I would—you know; things you do in bed when you're alone.

Yeah, all friendly. They were better company than Joe ever was. And I didn't have to smell 'em or listen to 'em rant or sleep with 'em. . . . Except for Leonard. Leonard was the bad one; I think he's from the devil because he keeps telling me to hurt people. I try not to listen, of course, what do you think? You think I like hurting people? Especially my kids?

The first time was on the bus coming from work, packed like always. This fat man squeezing in next to me, holding the overhead bar. He smelled awful and I started to say but then I heard Leonard. He told me to jab him in the armpit with my fingers, like that. (GESTURES) Well, it seemed wrong; I could have just asked him to move or something, but Leonard kept on saying "do it, do it." So, to shut him up if nothing else, I did. (REPEATS THE GESTURE) Nothing happened at all. The guy just said "Excuse me," and moved away. I was surprised how easy it was. And kind of funny, too; his face looked like a monkey.

Well, Leonard hung around a lot after that. I hit other people by accident on purpose. I pushed people into the street. I tripped an old man on his walker. Things like that. . . . Nobody got hurt, they just got mad; and they always looked so funny when they did; they looked like monkeys.

Then he started in on the boys. "Put pepper in their milk." "Switch the socks in their drawers." At first I said "No, they're just kids!" But he kept on and on and so just to shut him up, I put pepper in Willy's milk. Oh, god, was it ever funny! His eyes got big, he started sneezing, milk coming out of his nose. He just made it to the john before he up-chucked. Well, then I was sorry so I made him some brownies instead. And when I sewed up Mikey's pants, so when he went to put his leg in, he fell over. He looked like a monkey, it was hysterical. Well, then I was sorry so I made him angel food cake.

It went on like that, little funny things. But then Leonard told me to stick their heads under in the bathtub. Not to drown 'em, no; just to watch 'em squirm and all. Well, for a long time I kept saying no. I mean, suppose something went wrong? They were my kids, if I didn't have them, I wouldn't have anybody. But Leonard kept on. And the other voices weren't any help, I can tell you that. Suddenly they were quiet. I turned the TV up louder, I went around talking to myself, but nothing worked. He kept on and he kept on, so to finally shut him up, I did it. With Willy first. I stuck his head under, and he started kicking and twitching, he looked like a monkey, and then I—It all went wrong, of course. He died. . . . I think Leonard planned that all along. Right from the start, right from the guy on the bus. Thank God Mickey ran out, to the neighbor. . . . Well, I had to call Joe. Son of a bitch or not, they were still his kids, he had to know. He broke down, I could hear him crying and screaming and swearing; that felt good. It felt good to know he was miserable for one stinking time in his life.

Well, except for that, of course I felt like crap. It was intolerable. I couldn't live with myself. It's still hard talking about it.

Yes, but you need to talk about it, Mrs. Emerson. It's important for you to look at it carefully. After all, clearly the voices come from somewhere, there must be some reason you call them up. Especially—oh, by the way, I hope you don't mind if I smoke while you talk; it's a terrible habit, I know, but I can't seem to stop. Okay. Where were we?

You were telling me how Leonard told you to hurt Willy. And, please if you can, slow down. You talk so fast my notes just look like scribbles and I can't read them the next day. Now, tell me again: what were the exact words Leonard said to you?

###

ROSE, the Philanthropist

All I'm asking is a simple business deal. You accept my check and I offer a few conditions. We're talking three hundred million dollars for a brand new medical facility: it's not chicken soup. So what does it matter where it comes from? And why is it so crazy the Virgin Mary should talk to me? Because I'm Jewish? What, she wasn't? If you ask me, the woman finally had it with peasants. She appears to an illiterate French girl who can't even read; how could *she* improve the world? Make better cows? Or that shiksa Joan. Why should Mary give a hoot if France and England are friends or not? No. You find a widow with a fortune: that's how you change the world.

The first time I saw her was *Pesach*. I'm hosting a seder, and we come to it's time for Elijah's cup. We pour out a glass of wine, we open a door, and make a prayer the messiah should finally come. It's always a little spooky. You never know: it could actually happen. So there we are, we're singing:

"Eliyahu ha-Navi; Eliyahu ha-Tishbi , Eliyahu, Eliyahu, Eliyahu, ha-Giladi . . ."
And all of a sudden I hear from the garden somebody singing the rest:

Bimhayrah v'yamenu, yavo aleynu, im Mashiach ben David.

And this voice that's singing it, it's like nothing I ever heard. So out I go out for a look and there she is, sitting by the pool. "Hello," I says. And she says "*Shalom*, Rayzeleh. I'm the mother of God and He wants you should do Him a favor." In Yiddish, mind you, the whole conversation's in Yiddish. What? You're surprised the Virgin Mary speaks Yiddish? As the mother of God, shouldn't she know everything? Of course I don't believe her; in business you always look under the table. So I ask her, "Prove it. Do me a miracle or something." She says, "*Nu*, I'm here, I'm talking to you, that's not enough? Say yes or no." But I also know from business how not to be a shlemiel. So we talk.
What does she look like? Everybody who ever tried to write or paint failed. She's not this pure angelic *shayne punim* you think. No. She's got lines, she's got shrewd eyes, she's got character. She looks like Eleanor Roosevelt, only Jewish.

So she offers me the deal. She'll help me make more money than even God has, and all I have to do is promise how to use it. That's the catch: with all this money I have to build hospitals. In every place where there's hopeless diseases and suffering, she wants there should be a hospital and they should each one have the name of a saint from Saint Aaron all the way down to St. Zoticus.

I ask her of course, "Shouldn't they have Yiddish names? Avram, Benyomin, Dovid." She smiles at me like I'm the village idiot. "Who would believe the Virgin Mary appearing to a Yiddish-speaking businesswoman in Manhattan? After all, what does it matter what you call it so long as it works."

So this is where the hospitals came from. It helped of course that she has a direct line to the Biggest Inside Trader of them all, not to mention being the inventor of the universe. So yes: that's how I invent the Microrobotic Voice-Controlled Visiphonic Microwave Oven. How I create Sophia, the Bipolar Fashion Doll. How I start Uncle Moshe's Kosher Drive-Throughs. Everything I touch turns into capital gains. And hospitals spring up like weeds.

But now comes the hard part. One day, Mary tells me God has a test for me. That's the real catch. It so happens I had a son named Isaac. You'll recall there was another person once with a son named Isaac and you remember the test God gave to him. Mine's the same, only different. Suddenly my boy gets sick. Testicular cancer. God does nothing by halves. And Mary brings me the deal: I can either have Isaac alive and well, or finish with all the hospitals. Simple as that. God will save the life of my son, or He will continue feeding me riches and building hospitals beyond imagining. One life against millions. Well, I love my son, but there are babies all over the world starving. The Baal Shem Tov says, "He who saves a life, saves the world." But the Baal Shem Tov was never a mother. I'm completely *fermished* by this. Until I think it through.

So here is my check for three hundred fifty million dollars. You will build the largest and most comprehensive medical center ever. It will be attached to the greatest research facility in the world. A gigantic battlefield against every disease known to humanity. And you will name it the Isaac Bernstein Humanitarian Center. And my Isaac will be the chairman of the board.

Yes, he's still alive. How so? Listen: I presented God with the logical fallacy of His position. The point of the deal was to save lives and cure diseases, and one of these diseases was the cancer Isaac had, so if Isaac died we would not have cured him but God had promised to cure him since he was included in the collective entity of "all," and which God had made no provisions for exceptions, so what God was trying to do was to do something and not to do something at the same time, which would have cancelled out the whole deal, which, since it was from the spirit of God, would have cancelled God as well, thereby exploding Him out of existence and when God had no answer for *that* dilemma He just gave in on all counts. So you can start breaking ground tomorrow.

Oh, one more thing. When I die, you will canonize me. That's right. I want to be the first Jewish saint.

###

MRS. WOODRUFF, the Accused

Wait. You have to hear my side, don't you?

. . . Sorry, your honor. I shouldn't have shouted. But I need the court to understand why I did what I did, why I'm asking for leniency.

In the first place, I did not molest Matthew. I saved him. He was a lonely, unhappy outcast; both his parents worked twenty-four-seven in their very high-end law firm, ignoring him; his life was awful. Invisible.

And school was worse. It's what happens when you're gifted. His IQ tops half the kids in his year totaled up together so you can imagine the cruel teasing he gets. By the time he came into my U.S history class, I already knew about him; and I was determined to help him. Because my life was like his. I'm smart, I'm an only child, honor student, all that. Plus fat, uncoordinated, no talent whatsoever, always invisible.

So when I saw Matthew's name on the class roster, I was thrilled. I could help him; I would succeed where others had failed. So when he walked into class that first day, I smiled at him, I said, "Welcome, Matthew. I'm Mrs. Woodruff, welcome to the past." He looked at me, then looked away. He never smiled: he just nodded and headed for the most isolated seat he could find. But I had seen the pain in his eyes and my heart broke.

I tried at first to build his confidence by calling on him, asking him the tough questions I knew only he could answer. Well that proved wrong almost immediately; I just gave the class more ammunition to throw at him. And they caught on; one day, I asked him something. There was a moment. And then somebody muttered under his breath: "Why don't you just fuck him and get it over with." Mathew got up and walked out of the room and came to see me after school. I had made things worse; I ought to be fired, he said all the horrible things to me that I had said to myself. And we both started crying, and in that moment I suddenly loved him. I loved his sorrow and his potential, his heartbreak and his brilliance, and in some way I loved his need for me. So I kissed him, slowly for fear he'd draw back. But he didn't. He returned my passion.

I told him to come to my house that night. Philip was out of town. He should tell his parents he was coming for some special tutoring. He giggled when I said that: "special tutoring." And then I loved him for that too—the gift of being silly.

Well, so it happened. And continued to happen. I won't go into details, the prosecuting attorney has given us enough pornography for one day. But it wasn't just sex. It was evrything else that goes with love. We talked nonstop:—politics, books, secrets from our past—and we were silent too. Those wonderful silences where nobody has to talk.

Sure enough, he started to change for the good. He became less shy with me. He started initiating our dates: he would decide when we'd meet, he'd arrange the details. He grew more assertive. And he started changing in school too. He moved closer to the front. He started making little jokes, mostly they were dirty but at least they were jokes. And in his other classes too: I heard he was arguing more in English; he'd taken to correcting Mr.

Weiner in calculus. He even started looking people in the eye. It was lovely. My dream for him was working.

But then things turned. He started making demands. He had bought some book on Kama Sutra positions and insisted we try every one. He started to ask me questions in class that he knew I couldn't answer. He demanded that I write his English lit papers for him. He stopped turning in my assignments and demanded I give him high grades for work he never did, or else he'd tell. You see what I had done? I was the star of some film noir of my own making.

Why didn't I call it off? In the first place, he wouldn't let me. And in the second, I have to confess, I was taking a sort of perverse pride in what I had done. No matter that he became a sort of Frankenstein: it was I who had created it.

But it came to a crisis last month. We were in my kitchen, going over a paper I'd written for him on *The Scarlet Letter*. Strangely appropriate, don't you think? Philip was in the living room, watching CNN. And suddenly, Mathew says, "Let's fuck, right here, right now, on the kitchen table." I protested, Philip was just the other side of the door. But he insisted. He grabbed me, pushed me down. I told him to stop, I tried not to shout. "Show me how much you love me," he said. "The danger will bring us closer together, or else you know what I'll do." Well, what choice did I have? And, yes: it was in its own way, sort of wonderful. I remember in the middle of it, Philip called out, "You guys doing okay in there?" and Mathew called out, "Yes, Mr. Woodruff, we're doing great!" and we both just giggled and giggled and then we—well, you know.

So. This was my dilemma. I had succeeded where others had failed. I had done something everybody thought was undo-able. But at what price? So; there was only one thing left to do. So, this is the point, your honor. I may very well lose my license, spend time in jail, be branded all my life. And I'll be in the papers and the television news and everywhere. Famous in some bizarre fashion after all.

So that is why I called the police myself. I ought to get some points for that.

###

SALLY, the Victim

Don't look at me like that; you have no right to judge me. You were never around, you have no idea what it was like. Of *course* I hated myself. The first time I hit her, I felt so ugly afterwards I wanted to hide. No, you listen. I want you to hear every part of it. I want you to know what it was like.

It was a Sunday night; I'd had a long, horrible day at the restaurant so I was trying to nap before I started dinner. Mother was in her chair, with the TV blaring and she started whining again: "Sally, I'm wet. Sally I'm wet." Sure enough: her robe was soaked and she smelled awful. What is it with old people? You wash 'em and spray 'em, and they still stink? I said why didn't she call me sooner. "I can't help it," in that thin high noise like fingernails on a blackboard. "You don't try," I said. "You do this on purpose." I know it made no sense, but I was too angry. And then—right in front of me—she fouled herself; she couldn't wait two more minutes. "You did this on purpose, didn't you," I hollered at her. "Just to spite me." Where that came from, I have no idea; some long-held anger I suppose, for her getting sick and you bailing like you did. No, don't interrupt, you have no right to any opinion at all.

Something broke in me and I slapped her so hard my fingers tingled. She looked up at me, her eyes wide with fear, her mouth open, but nothing came out. "Now behave yourself!" And I went back to my room, shaking. I hated myself. Is that what you want to hear?

But after that, it got easier.

Like I wrote you, her condition got worse. Her strength, her life—dribbling away drop by drop. And you never answered my letters; you couldn't care less. Don't interrupt, I don't want to hear your lies.

Of course she belonged in some rest home where she could get care and I wouldn't have to be her prisoner. How could I afford it? Even cashing in her insurance, too many doctors, too many meds. A fucking day-care nurse. And you were invisible, buried somewhere in the Army overseas. You were always overseas. I realized one day it was on purpose. You bailed and left me stuck with the zombie, with her whining and her incoherent babblings and her smell and her medications and me counting pennies and having no life of my own, and so I hit her. And I hit her again.

Her condition got worse; I grew desensitized. Soon I had to fire the day care; I couldn't risk her seeing the bruises. So that meant I had to leave her in the house alone while I worked. But then the real nightmares started. Like the time I came home and she was on the kitchen floor crying in pain, her leg all red and puckering. She'd tried to make herself some tea and spilled hot water all over herself. I sprayed it with Bactine and thought about taking her to an ER, but didn't because they would ask me questions. Or when she thought her meds were M&M's and nearly overdosed. Good thing I caught her before she did herself in.

Or the time I came home and found her gone. She'd wandered outside in her nightgown, looking for Dad. I was panicked, I thought what if she'd got hit by a car or something, although, in a way, I almost hoped she was. How's that for a daughter's love? I found her when I called the cops: somebody had brought her in. You can imagine the questions they asked me, like a criminal. They told me, if it ever happened again, they'd call social services to check on elder abuse.

There. That horrible thing that I was doing and getting more easy with, it had a name. Elder Abuse. But it's a shitty name, if you ask me, because it doesn't say who's abusing who. Because I kept having this notion that she was really sane after all. She was still there, that funny, sharp foxy lady we remembered, but for some evil reason, she was faking. No, shut up; you have no right to any opinion. And, of course, as the nightmare wore on, I made myself believe it. It gave me one more good excuse to hit her.

Things grew even worse of course. I put a safety lock on the door. I kept changing where I hid her meds. I put one of those monitoring bracelets on her, although I had to re-teach her every single day how to use it. But even so, she'd find new ways to get into trouble. So I had to start tying her down, like we were in some Nazi movie. I'd put her in her chair with a bucket at her feet, the remote in her lap, a sandwich and an apple on the table. And then I took a scarf and tied her to the chair. I didn't dare use a rope, it would leave burns.

Which of course meant that I couldn't stay away very long. I had to run back every couple of hours to make sure she was okay. So eventually they fired me. Who could blame them?

Then the worst of all. She started thinking I was you. Calling me Martin. "Martin, get me this; Martin do that." I said I was Sally, Martin was overseas. She said I was wrong, Sally was the one overseas and I was Martin and why was I wearing a dress and trying to confuse her? How do you think that made me feel? It was the last straw . . . no: not a straw. It was the knife. The last twist of the knife.

So that's why I did it. Why I washed her and cleaned her up and did her hair fine and fancy like a celebrity on parade. Untied her . . . left the meds out on the table . . . and went to the movies.

You do what you think best. I don't much care anymore. I'm just glad it's over.

###

SANDRA, the Writer

I've told you all this before; what's the point of going all over it again? Don't you take notes? Of course I'm upset. How long—.

(SHE nearly breaks down; stops and gets control of herself.)

I swore I wasn't gonna cry in here ever again. Okay. I'm in control. Where would you like me to start?

(SHE speaks to a presence in her head.)

Just a minute. I'm busy now.

Okay. You know how famous Becky Blue is. *Becky Blue and the Daring Rescue. Becky Blue and the Crystals of Time.* A half dozen more; best sellers every one. First time out; how lucky can you get. But the devil tempts you in all kinds of ways. I got the idea in college when I was taking a class in children's fantasy. Alice, Dr. Doolittle, the whole gang. I wondered if I could write something like that—a cute little winner that would earn me enough to write real literature. And *zap*: I was taking a shower at the time, I distinctly remember that—water always works for me. I heard her in my head. "Hello. I'm Becky Blue. I live on Freemon. It's a world on the other side of the sun. My dad was captured by Hostiles. Me and my cat Plato and my friend Charlie, we're going to find him. And then have lots of adventures. Will you write them all down if I tell them to you?"

Yes, that's what I heard. It was so clear that I actually spoke "Yes." And by the time I got dressed, the first book was in my head. The entire story from when they kidnapped Dad all the way to rescuing him from the prison island. I got to my computer, hoping I wouldn't forget, but the more I typed, the clearer it got. I could swear Becky was beside me, telling me what to write.

What? No, not now. I've already told about the Marnolians and the secret code.

Doc, keep asking me questions. It helps me focus.

Yes, and all the characters were there too. Charlie and his wild schemes that always work somehow. Plato the outlaw shape-shifter. The Wizard, Mrs. Dibble, Millie the inventor: a whole universe had popped into my head.

What did it feel like? Inspiration like that? It's scary as shit, that's what it is.

Just a minute, will you? Let me get this out.

Why is it scary? Because you don't know where it comes from; you or a person taking control of your mind. Who the hell is in charge? Of course I expected it to dry up eventually. At most I'd get some money out of it and then move on to real fiction. But it kept coming. Becky's personality fleshed out. Ideas rained constantly. Can you understand the horror I live with? Becky never shuts up. She's the one in charge.

Well of course I did. I tried writing all kinds of other stuff.

I already told about Speckles and the missing portrait. No. I already said outer space is out.

Sorry; what did you just ask, Doc? Yes, of course. A novel about adults with grown-up feelings. Sex: "She came and came in unending fountains of pleasure." Or death: "Momma's hand grabbed mine as though I were her lifeline." One great discovery. "Suddenly Maria Theresa knew what it was the Holy Mother required of her."

It IS great. You're just a piker. Bread and butter? Screw you; there's more to life than bread and butter. I tried giving you a boyfriend. You didn't want him taking over. Shut up; just shut up for one hour.

Oh, now she's crying. I can't stand it when she cries. *Stop crying.* Ask me something, Doc. Please. I could send her into outer space and there could be a meteor; the hull could be punctured, they could all—*Stop crying.*

And of course she's right about the other part. She *does* pay the bills. The movie rights alone are obscene. But is it worth it, to go through life like this? Not to be in charge—

Venus? How will you get there? No, the Wizard doesn't have that kind of power.

Doc, Doc, help me. Throw me a lifeline. I just want my own mind back. A day, one fucking hour.

The powder? No, we used all the Green Powder in The Adventure of the Mountains. *It would have to be something more scientific. Mrs. Dibble has relatives on Venus? How the hell did she . . . ? Oh, that would work, that would work.*

Doc, Doc, wait a minute, will you.

You mean all this time Mrs. Dibble was an alien? Wait, lemme get this.

(SHE takes out writing pad and scribbles as the lights fade out.)

The GPP? Galactic Peace Patrol . . . Yes; they're coming after Plato; that crime he committed. . . .

###

STEPHANIE, the Realist

I'm holding Ginny close. Her baby head swivels until she finds the nipple. She feeds in loud sucking noises that sound like music, and I swear she looks up at me and winks. She's nervous. It's her first recital. Her tutu doesn't fit right. I'm desperately trying to pin it around her waist while her eyes are blinking because "ballerinas don't cry," but I accidentally stick her and she cries and I hold her and tell her, "I'm sorry but Daddy and Mommy don't like each other anymore and it has nothing to do with you," but now she won't look up at me, but turns the pages of her book, *Where the Wild Things Are.* She clutches it while Paul comes down the stairs with his suitcase and she runs to him and begs him not to go away. But he does, he's gone; she runs up to her room and closes the door. Her stereo starts blasting with a throbbing bass that drives you crazy and she comes downstairs followed by her giggling chums and now they want brownies but it's eleven o'clock at night so we pile into the station wagon and drive out to the all-night Steak 'n Shake which is crowded to the gills with everybody from the home team which has just won and all the cheerleaders. "*V-I-C-T-O-R-Y, Come on men of Stanley High*" and they're making a three-tiered pyramid and Ginny's the top but she's having trouble getting up there. They're starting to wobble and I want to run out and help but I know if I do that, she won't talk to me again for weeks and I've been through THAT little drama before and anybody who doesn't know what hell is like has never lived through their daughter going through puberty; world war three doesn't compare with buying her first bra which she refuses to wear because it's an out-dated custom foisted on liberated women by men who are afraid of women with large boobs. But then, when she puts on her prom dress and comes down the stairway where her date stands, all tuxedo-ed and clean shaven and holding the corsage in his hand like it's a five-foot anaconda, your heart breaks. They stay out all night at this massive pajama party. I hope it's supervised, but we've had that talk and I have to trust her. But when she comes back from her first semester at college she's different. It's not just the hair which is now orange, but there's a slight firmness to her cheekbones, a little wispy smile on the corners of her lips, and she walks a little bit more solid and I can only wonder who the boy was that made her a woman. Of course I can't ask her, although that night at supper, I gently touch her cheek and she looks at me and winks and we know everything about everything and it's wonderful. She won't marry him, she's going to be independently wealthy because I'm sure some part of her resents all the things she couldn't have because her Mom juggled two jobs and By All The Saints In The Bible She Will Never Be That Poor. I love the look in her eyes when she says things like that, because I know underneath she's as terrified as I was. However, she shows me his picture while we're putting up window dressings on her first apartment, so I know that she at least has love. It's a horrible one-room studio she's renting in the worst neighborhood of the city, but "It's cool, Mom, it's near the bus." And, of course, when I offer to help her out every month, she looks at me with murder in her eyes. But then, so I won't be worried, she shows me the pistol she's bought with part of the graduation money from her father. She says, "See that bird on that tree out the window, that robin that won't shut up," and she takes aim and fires and the bird's head is suddenly gone. She blows into the muzzle and grins, she flexes her muscles, she turns and there's this goon coming after her. I'm trying to help, but my legs won't move, it's like I'm moving through cheesecake. She grabs him by the arm, flips him, he falls bam! on his back and she puts one foot on his belly and raises her arm in triumph and the stadium goes wild with applause. She's won the gold medal! Bless her heart: all those years in ballet class and the cheering squad paid off because now she can call her own shots. They want her to endorse tennis shoes, but she just walks away, turning her back on all of that fame and fortune and I'm so proud of her, she gets into the limo and drives away. And I can't let go, I just can't let go, so I fly after them. I look down on the car as it speeds onto the expressway and merges into traffic. It's hard for me to keep up, my wings are as old as my knees but I manage. Now I can see inside the car. She's in the back seat, putting on makeup, she's late for a photo call. "Slow the car down," I call out. Of course she doesn't listen to me, but just looks up at me and smiles. And now there's this big gaping hole in the bridge and the car plunges into the river. It bobs up and down on the water like apple-dunking in Halloween thing and then it starts to go under. I fly down, I dive. I barely catch up with it as I swim harder, faster. We both reach the bottom at the same time. I can see her looking at me through the window. She's trying to open the door. I'm trying too. It won't budge. I pound. She slaps at it from inside. I have a hammer in my hand and I smash it against the window but . . . the hammer's made of chocolate and it melts as I watch. And now I can see the water rising inside. She looks at me, she looks up at me and it's like she's at my breast again and she looks up at me and she winks and then it's all black and—.

What? Oh, I must have dozed. Yes. I'm ready. No, I haven't changed my mind. I simply can't have this child. Please don't try to talk me out of. Please don't try to talk me out of it. Please don't try to talk me out of it.

(SHE continues as Lights Fade.)

###

CERES, the Baker

You don't mind if I work while we talk? I have to get three loaves done by six. Where to start? I guess when Carlos died. Somehow I thought he was eternal. Always smiling and making jokes; like when we had to put Groucho down. When the vet took him, Carlos said to me, "Do you suppose there's a god for dogs? And if so, how do they pray to it? Maybe that's what all that sniffing each other's butts is really about!" I laughed so hard that gunk came out of my nose

So when he died, it was like the end of the world. People were wonderful at first, but later they stopped coming around. But I didn't mind. I hated their silly chatter about stupid things. After you've buried the center of your life, *everything* is stupid. Television was awful; I gave up reading; I stopped all my subscriptions. Somehow Martha Stewart and the color of kitchen towels didn't much matter. I hit bottom when I realized I hadn't even taken a bath in a week and that awful smell in the house was me.

But it was then, while I was soaking in the tub, my life changed. I was leafing through some old *Martha Stewart Living* when a page caught my eye: "Baking Bread Is Easier Than You Think." Now, you have to know this about me: in your wildest dreams I am nobody's idea of a cook. I had to buy a book called *Boiling Water for Dummies*, and even that was confusing. My idea of making dinner was ordering Chinese instead of pizza. Carlos, now he could make a grilled hot dog taste like filet mignon. So I let him cook and we were both happy.

And, of course, all this time while I was in perpetual mourning, I was eating crap. Frozen dinners, carry-out—there were days I had cereal three meals in a row and for dessert I'd have an apple. So normally, *Baking Bread Is Easier Than You Think* would have just gone by me. But there in the tub, something made me read it all the way through.

And it actually sounded like something I could even do. And who would know if I screwed up? I could always eat the mistakes, right? So out I went to buy the whole store: bread flour, yeast, eggs, sugar, bowls, a 200-dollar mixer with a dough hook. An apron that said "Don't fuck around with the cook!" I was Chef Boy-ar-dee in drag. And, as fate would have it, I saw a flier posted at the Kroger: "Baking Bread Classes for Beginners." Now, I'm by no means a religious person, but it did all seem like more than coincidence. Maybe Carlos was sending me a message.

So I took the beginner's class, and then I took more classes and I bought books. Ethnic breads. Dessert breads. Vegan Breads. I learned all the secrets. I learned how powdered yeast is different from instant-rise yeast, which is different from cake yeast. I learned that there's bread flour, there's all-purpose flour, there's bleached and unbleached and whole-wheat flour; there's rye, and spelt, millet and polenta, quinoa and buckwheat, the names were like music.

I learned how to test the water temperature with my pinky. I learned how to knead dough like making pottery. I learned the poke test, which is when you poke the dough and if it bounces back it's risen. (I remember thinking it was like Carlos: when I poked him to see if he was ready, he would, excuse my French, have risen too.) I learned how to shape round loaves, long loaves, how to braid. I was the Michelangelo of grains: what was the "David" compared to my six-stranded challah?

And my soul expanded too. My heart woke up. I discovered that the fifteen minutes I spent kneading was like psychotherapy: there you are, you and the bread somehow connected, you thinking of nothing but the texture of the dough under your hands—it was like zen. I even found out I could almost be happy again.

Until I suddenly realized what I was really doing. I was making all this bread for Carlos. In case he wasn't really dead, and one day he'd come home from work and I'd show him the bagels I'd made and we'd have them with a couple of shmears for breakfast. I remember I was working on my first Schiacciata con L'Uva at the time and it was like he died all over again. I felt cold, dizzy, I had to lie down and cry it all out one more time.

Of course I stopped baking. I went back to being my former miserable self. But this time, what it took was a story in the local paper, about this group cooking meals for shut-ins—ailing or infirm; or locked away in old-people's homes; people as lonely as I was. And—believe me, I know it's weird—I started to laugh. The same force or thing or ghost who'd opened the Martha Stewart to the right page, and who led me to the flier in the grocery store—this same blessed thing was talking to me again. And I knew this time who it was.

So this is how I became what I am now: a goddess of grains spreading nourishment around the city. I bake all day; I donate to a dozen places. I'm Florence Nightingale with crumbs. Am I happy? Thank God, yes. And have I learned anything to pass on to you? Of course; what are old people for?

What is the main ingredient in bread that makes the flour work? It's the yeast, of course. And did you realize that yeast is a living thing? It sits in the envelope like a bear hibernating through the winter. You put it in warm water with some honey to wake it up, and then you pour it into the flour, it starts to eat. When you knead it, what you're doing is feeding it, so it grows bigger and richer all the time. It's life, you see what I mean? And when you eat it, you're eating a slice of life.

Ach, look at me: I'm talking and talking and I'm forgetting my manners. Here's a loaf I made fresh this morning. Would you like a piece?

###

Sense of finding belonging
Jewish
Recovering past family memories and facts

HELEN, the Daughter

I am standing in the middle of a small cemetery outside the Polish village of Versheznyu. It's very nowadays, although before the Holocaust it was a thriving Jewish community, something like *Fiddler on the Roof* only different. There, all the Jews had to leave, but at least they were still alive.

I see around me many small headstones crowding against each other; many need repair; nearly all are impossible to read. The particular grave I'm standing at belongs to Mirele Shaynah Rifknowski

(MEER-e-luh SHAY-nuh Riff-NOV-ski)

Or, in English: Miriam Sharon Rifknowski. Although when her daughter—that would be my mother—when she came to America, she changed her surname to Richards, and eventually married a man named McDougal. Yes, my mother married a gentile. As did I. No particular reason; I'm sure it doesn't mean anything. Standing here I feel a sense of repose, as though I had walked into the first room I had as a child and my Raggedy Ann was still smiling at me. Somehow I belong at this grave.

Which is what I came all the way from Ohio to find out. About a year ago, when I was going through my mother's things after the funeral, I found an old scrapbook: dried-up pages with small Kodaks pasted between old letters and wedding invitations and things nobody has the courage to throw away. My mother had labeled most of the photos, so the family history was pretty intact. Now this struck me as odd, you know, because, having married out of the faith, what was she so anal about? I mean, she never hid the fact that she was Jewish, and therefore, so was I, but she kept quiet and celebrated Christmas with Pop's family. So in the scrapbook, was she regretting somehow? Did she secretly feel guilty?

Because here they were: Uncle Jacob, Aunt Sadie's second brother who married Sophie and moved to California. Martha and Gertie Shmulke, twins from Abe and Golda Hersholt. Sarah: Grandpa Moshe's second daughter who fell from a horse. It was like reading a novel by James Michener. And then: a wedding photo labeled "Mirele Hersholt married Meyer Krakovnu." A typical entry, except to this was added three words: "She survived Auschwitz."

I was frozen. Even 60 years after the fact, the words still send shivers through you. And to suddenly realize that somebody in my family nearly died there. Why hadn't my mother told me? And what happened? I mean, they had children, I'm proof of that—why were the children spared? Were they taken in by gentiles? Were they at all in the camps? I called my Aunt Sadie. "Oh yes, it's true," she said. "Your grandparents—may they rest in peace—were martyrs. But your parents were hidden by some French family until after the war, when they went to England, and then your mother came to America and changed her name so it got all fermished." But why hadn't anybody ever told me? "Ach," she said, "it's all in the past, let them rest, and move on already." "How can I do that? I have to connect." "Then go visit the grave, I think it's still there. Get it out of your system."

Get it out of my system? Impossible. You can't escape your history, can you? I couldn't sleep. There was such a tumult in my head, my husband, Andrew, he finally said "Go. Stop driving yourself crazy." That's Andrew for you; he can't understand why this would be important. "If you were Jewish," I tell him, "You would know what it means." "How long has it been since you were Jewish?" he barks and goes back to checking his daily stock results.

So I came here seeking I don't know what. It's getting chilly; I should leave but I can't. My thoughts wander. Her gravestone is here, but there is none next to it. So Meyer maybe died in the camps. She must have loved him, although he was probably chosen for her. Maybe she was lucky and got somebody wonderful. She kept house, she cooked three meals a day, she raised two children. I wonder if she liked cooking; making shabbos bread and all. The house must have smelled warm and sweet, like birthdays; she must have had that smell in her head all her life. Was she happy despite being poor? After all, she was keeping alive a house. She was feeding my mother. She was, in her own way, praising God.

I try to be in her life. She gets up early and makes some tea. She checks her yeast cultures. She goes out to buy her flour and sugar and butter. She stops to rest by that bridge, with the sun on her face. She meets with friends and they gossip and maybe they wonder what's happening with the Germans across the border. But then why didn't they leave? Maybe they couldn't. Maybe she didn't want to. After all, he had a town, a past, a whole world. So many connections like a soft overcoat. And when Meyer came home from his work, she must have been happy to see him. "He's smiling; it was a good day. We'll have a nice supper. He'll say his prayers, he'll read his books, we'll talk a little, he'll take me to bed." They always had bed, didn't they? Good times, bad times, whatever, they could always make a little love.

Who took care of her after the war? She's feeble; she forgets to eat. She sits in the chair and stares at the sky, until she can't even get out of bed. She lays there and watches her memories. Maybe, like I do when I can't sleep, she picks a year of her life and tries to remember every single wonderful thing that happened then. She takes long naps, and then one comes along that she just doesn't wake up from. Maybe until now.

Are you here, Mirele? What do I do now?

###

SHARON, the Painter

All my life has been my work of art, created out of breath and vision and will. I sit here now, at the end of it, surrounded by images of every painting and sketch I ever drew. I want you to choose one to have after I'm gone.

The first one I remember was a princess climbing a mountain in her wedding dress. I don't recall why she was undergoing such a strenuous challenge on the happiest day of her life; perhaps even then I knew fairy tales don't always end happily. And I remember there was a great big yellow sun at the top and also thin strong lines on a diagonal which was rain. My mother said, "Darling, you can't have it raining and sunny at the same time." And I said, "Yes I can, because even if the sun is shining here, it's probably raining someplace else." And she said, "Oh, so your picture is about the whole world then, is it?" And I thought to myself: "Of course; aren't they all?" But I didn't say that out loud because somehow I knew that she wouldn't understand.

And another thing happened then. I cut my finger and a drop of blood dripped onto the paper which somehow blended into the color of the mountainside, giving the gray and brown rocks an odd magenta color that somehow gave the picture a new heightened intensity; the rocks looked like they were alive, attacking the princess. "Of course they're alive," I thought. "They have my blood in them."

I drew dozens of princesses after that. In jeweled gowns, going to dances. In jeans, playing on monkey bars. In uniforms, as nurses or astronauts. But all flawed in some fashion, ruining them for me, until one day, this princess was climbing a fire truck ladder to save her dog from the top floor, a golden retriever, like Jacki was. Again, somehow I cut my finger and a drop of blood fell on the orange-yellow cones that were the flames. And, as before, some indescribable synergy happened between the medium and the blood, giving the fire that same heightened intensity as the rocks had, as though it were alive. It was then I made the decision that shaped my process forever after.

Every painting in my life since then, every painting that mattered for one reason or another, perhaps they hurt the most—I would find a way to enrich one of the colors with a drop of my own blood.

The painting that won me my first blue ribbon in high school was a horse rearing up to throw off its rider. There was blood in the panic in the horse's eyes. The painting that got me admitted to the Art Institute School was an old woman sitting on the top of her house in the center of a large umber plain: She's looking to the far horizon, where a faintly lit brick tower juts up into the scarlet sky. The light is obviously death glowing amber and blood. The one that got me a Cunningham grant, *Floral Nightmare?* . . . Yes, in the roses.

And then there was the painting that cost me David. David Trelawney, the boy I fell in love with in Paris when we were there on grants. We spent all our time together those months, working side by side; a study in contrasts. I loved the painting, he loved the results; I was content with my life, teaching and creating. He was driven by a fierce hunger for fame. At the time, I was working on studies for what eventually turned out to be *In Advance, Number Three*. He was trying to shape some vision in his head, trying to create a whole new school: Kandinsky by way of Wyeth with a touch of Klee—those are his words, not mine. You can see how bound for failure he was. But we didn't know that then; we were young lovers whose days were lost in the agony of creating. Me, in my slow, molasses-like deliberate way, getting maybe three or four good brush strokes an hour. He, slapping on colors in a frenzy of speed and frustration. I can still hear him muttering to his canvas: swearing at it when it refused to cooperate, cajoling it when it gave only a little, singing to it when it cooperated.

At night we made wonderful love. He was inventive and caring, listening to my breathing and responding. I often thought if he'd put as much invention into his art as he did to his love, he'd be unparalleled. But of course I never told him. Why spoil it when I knew it would end soon enough?

And it did, as I feared it would. I had finally conquered the painting. I had the Madonna just so: her face with the exact expression of fear and love in her eyes. I had the Christ child in her arms, looking up at her for comfort against the pain in the world. I had the black thunderclouds looming beyond the window. And I knew where the blood would go. There, in the eyes of the doomed young man, who had tasted the world so far and found it bitter. And it made the painting brilliant, as I knew it would.

I didn't show it to David for a long time, but when he finally saw it, he stared at it and said nothing. And then he turned to me, tears in his eyes, and he shook his head, and he lifted up his arms in some awful gesture of want, and walked out of the studio. No, I didn't follow him. Nor did I try to find him when he never came back. I knew better. I tore apart his half-finished attempts to revolutionize the art world, sold off his tools, and burnt his sketchbooks.

Why did I do it, you ask? Do you mean why did I destroy his unfinished detritus, or why did I put the blood in the painting, knowing what would be the result?

Oh, you child with so much to learn. You generous, loving, and foolish lad, who looks at the world as a place of comfort. Who sees in art that sweet narcotic of pleasure it was never meant to be. How could I not? What good would it have been? Yes, of course. You understand. There has to be blood.

So, my love, now you know my secret, which one do you want?

###

KALI-YA , the Warrior

So, you want to write a book about me? You would like to know how I became ruler of the galaxy; how I clawed and scratched my way to the Supreme Throne? But, please, have a glass of brandy while we talk. I insist. It's very rare, you know, from Earth. I have the last bottles left in the universe. People have murdered for less. So. Where to begin?

First I had to become strong. I was born a puny little girl on Antares Seven, the pleasure planet. My parents ran the most expensive dens and brothels; they had every luxury that greed could buy. But they were soft. They spent their days at work and their nights in their drug-induced fantasies. I hated them; I feared I would one day become them

So I ran away. I stowed aboard an outplanet trader but soon I was caught, and spent the rest of the voyage sweating in the nuclear furnaces. Lifting and loading Power Cylinders 10 hours a shift and fighting off the apes who tried to rape me every night. I grew strong; I learned to fight, making my arms and legs my weapons. One ugly pig never left me alone, baiting and insulting me. One day I threw a bottle of solvent acid into his face. While he was on the floor, screaming and kicking, I plunged a knife into his neck. We all stood in a circle and watched him die. After that, they left me alone.

Are you enjoying the brandy? Yes, I thought you would. Have another. Good.

Now I was strong I had to become smart. First I sold myself on Trymok Two; I had learned many useful things in my father's brothels. Of course I became a whore; how else do you study men? One night I recognized one of my customers as a high-class politician. Blackmail was easy. He made me his first assistant. Watching him in negotiations, I learned how to read faces and bodies: how the twitch of an eyebrow meant you were winning; how to let your opponent lose and still save face, turning him into your ally. I remember how the fool would test me every so often, letting slip information I was not supposed to have, and waiting to see what I would do with it. But I never betrayed him. I simply waited.

And then, of course, as the years went by, he grew sloppy. So, when the Reptonion Crisis developed, I was ready. You remember that time, don't you? When the Outer Planets rebelled against the Consortium, when Yu Chen and his armies threatened an alliance with the Repton Triumvirate and my mentor was called in to negotiate a treaty? And of course you remember the Hanover Letter: the document that proved he was secretly promising the Reptons total control of the UpReach trade routes in exchange for 75per cent of the profits? Do you remember how he protested the signature was a forgery? And the testimony of his daughter: when she swore that she had seen her evil Daddy in bed with Yu Chen's son, who in his turn was a triple agent for the Barbarian Detente? Yes, that was a time, wonderful days for a schemer like me. Governments fell, my mentor committed suicide. The Reptonion Triumvirate broke apart when one leader after another was assassinated. The economies of two hundred planets were ruined and when the dust settled two years later, the Barbarian Detente wound up in control of everything. And do you want to know the truth? He had been right all along: letter *was* forged. Of course it was me. I had already been secretly married to Yu Fong for years, waiting for this very chance. And it was me who poisoned his father to clear the way to power.

More brandy? I insist. I said I insist. I had power, but now I had to learn finesse. Playing one side against another, holding a third side as bait; carefully selected accidents; minor uprisings here and there. It's all so many games. The trick is to keep changing the rules.

And then I got lucky. The Dragons appeared. An advanced species with voracious appetites for human flesh. How many years and how many billions of lives were lost before we finally defeated them. I myself led the fleet at the Battle of Zeribus. Who else was there? And, yes: that's where Yu Fong died. History records his brave charge into the Fire Zone. But history lies. My husband didn't die in the battle. He died one hour before it began. I know because I killed him. You can't rule galaxies unless you rule them alone. I shot him, placed his body in the Cruiser and blew it apart to make it look like death in battle. I gave him a hero's funeral and I emerged from the war triumphant. I reluctantly let the populace crown me empress and humbly allowed them to place my bony rear end onto the Supreme Throne. I became the wonder woman that you came to see today; this warrior goddess you want to write a book about.

So my life became as you see it now. I control the fates of a thousand worlds. The decisions I make alter the course of history. It is all so much child's play. But it's also dull beyond belief. Now I know why God threw the Devil out of Heaven, making an enemy of him. God had to do something to make existence a little bit interesting. That's why I agreed to see you. Don't you wonder about that? After all, I've had many offers to write it all down; why do you think I would want to tell it to you?

What is that? You're feeling dizzy? Cold? Of course it's the brandy. What do you think? Can you imagine how small my life has become and how bored my days are? There are no worlds left to conquer; no enemies to defeat. I am surrounded by stupidity and I feel myself growing soft. So now and then I test myself. Am I hard enough inside? Is it still fun to watch a living thing turn into a corpse in front of me? Every death is a triumph for me. Even one as pathetic and useless as yours. Sleep in peace, you stupid fool.

###

BES, the Child

Popper says I'm his favorite princess. He gives me a huggy and when he picks me up, he makes a funny noise, like ooohf! and says "You're my favorite princess" and he says when they ordered me from the baby store, they asked for a princess that was special and that's what they got and it doesn't matter that I can't count or read or use the Johnny by myself because I can do things they can't, like make my color pictures. I make boxes and squiggles and circles and sometimes things I don't know what they are but they're fun and sometimes Popper looks at my colors and makes up a story about what he sees in them. Sometimes there are giants and sometimes Sponge Bob and sometimes other princesses and then he puts them on the wall and when Hannah comes to clean up and take me for a walk she says they're as pretty as a moosie-um, but I don't know what a moosie-um is, but it's probably good because she laughs when she says it. I like Hannah. Sometimes I pretend she's my Mommie.

My real Mommie went away a long time ago. Popper says she's in the sky. I ask him where in the sky and why can't I see her and he says, "Some day, when you grow up, I'll try to tell you." And guess what? Last night, when I asked him, he said, "Okey-dokey" and he got me out of bed and put my coat on over my pee-jays and then he took me for a long ride in the car. It was dark, and we went a long way and then we got out and it was warm and Popper told me to look up. And I did and saw a gazillion little lights hanging up there. Popper said, "Those are stars, Princess. Aren't they pretty?" and I said they were and he told me that people lived up in the stars. After you live down here for a time, something happens to you and you change and you turn into stars and live up in the sky.

And he pointed here and there and told me that you could see some of the people. There's a man with a bo-narrow and a queen and a man who's a horse too. That would be funny but I know Popper only made that up. There's a woman with a big glass of water. And a big strong man named Herklees.

And then he showed me where Mommy was. She joined another family up there; there were—I forgot how many but they're sisters. More than one hand, but not two hands. I asked Popper why Mommy wanted to live with her sisters in the sky instead of with us and then he just blinked his eyes real hard and said he didn't know. He said sometimes people are happier living in the sky. I couldn't guess why because it's always dark and cold up there.

Then Popper said no; it just looked like it was cold and dark, but when you get there, it's warm and good. You can tell because of all the lights. When you get there you never feel like crying inside, and everybody likes you and you get a huggy whenever you want one. I asked him if he was going to change and go live up there with Mommy and he said not for a long long time. And I said could I go too because I didn't want to be by myself and he said of course because I was his favorite princess. Then he gave me and Raggedy Ann a real big huggy and we got back in the car and Popper gave me some cocoa-milk and I fell asleep on the way home.

And I had a dream. A dream is when you sleep and the Queen of the Fairies comes into your head and turns on the telly-vision and makes up a story just for you.

And this was the best dream I ever had. Me and Raggedy Ann and Popper and Mommy were by a big house and we were all holding hands and dancing and the little dog was there and he danced with us but then he changed and he was a prince and he started singing and he was singing "Little Town" like when Jesus was born and then it was snowing like when you got some on your tongue it tasted like candy and we ate and laughed and it wasn't dark and cold at all; it was warm and light like Popper told me and we all flew up together—right there into the sky—and we went to visit all the people in the stars. The man with the bo-narrow showed me how to use it and then the lady with the glass of water gave us some but it was leminade. And then the man who was also a horse told us he would give us a ride if we gave him some leminade and we did and he gave us a ride to the big house where all the sisters live but before we got there a big monster like a snake was chasing us and the man who was also a horse was riding as fast as he could and then Herklees was there and he stepped on the snake and made him all mush and then we went into the house and there was all the sisters she lived with and each one was so pretty and so nice I could see why Mommy liked living with them. Then we had cookies and the prince made us laugh and even Raggedy Ann laughed and this time you could hear her fine and then the Queen came in and gave us big hamburgers. And Mommy's was so big she couldn't finish it so she gave some of it to me. Then she leaned down and her eyes were shiny and then she started to tell me something but I woke up and we were home and Popper was carrying me into the house.

And I told Popper all about my dream and he gave me a huggy and said sometimes the dreams that the Queen of the Fairies shows us one day actually happen. But I said I didn't know what it was that Mommy was going to say to me before I woke up. And Popper said, "I bet she told you she loved you." And I said, "How do you know?" And he said, "Because I want to believe it. Don't you want to believe it too?" And then he gave me some more coco-milk and I went to bed. I hoped I would have the same dream and Mommy would get to tell me what she started to say, but he said maybe one day I will, he's sure as shooting sure about that.

And he's prob'ly right. Because I believe it.

###

EMILY, the Mourner

So, what are you gonna do? We're running late; you coming with or not? You gonna sit in your room with your Playstation, your computer games, your *Star Trek* posters like some crybaby or join your Dad and me like a person and get in the car? Do I have to pick you up and drag you? I can do it, you're eleven but I can still lift you.

I don't wanta get mad, I shouldn't have to treat you like a crybaby but when you sit here and act like one, what am I supposed to do? Because there's no way you're not going: She was your grandma, you owe it to her. She was good to you: she gave you presents you didn't deserve—who bought you that Playstation in the first place, who took you out of school against your mother and me—and took you to see *Star Wars* in the afternoon? You come and respect her memory; show gratitude for her life. That's not hard to understand, is it, so what's going on, what are you afraid of?

Because I think that's what's at the bottom of this; you're afraid of something. But come on: what? She's gonna jump out of the coffin and run around the chapel? Dance a hora through the aisles? Because she's not, you know. She's not even gonna be there. What's there, what's lying in that coffin, that isn't even her, it's just, I don't know, a shell. It's only death, you don't have to be afraid. I understand that, believe me. I was afraid too. I got over it. Listen: I was sitting in the waiting room in the hospital, it was midnight or something, when the nurse came out. "Mrs. Nomberg, she's passed, I'm sorry," and I thought *what? passed?'* It sounded like moving from one class to another, like she was leaving kindergarten and going into first grade, and I didn't understand how that related to my mother.

And then I was alone in the little room and there she was on the bed. What should I do? I was never this close before. Your grandpa died when I was in the service and I never even got back for the funeral. So this was a whole new scary thing for me. I looked down on the bed. It looked like my mother, but her face was skinnier, smoother, I can't describe it. I stared at her chest for a long time, *maybe she'll take a breath, she's just sleeping real deep and they just* think *she's gone, and I'll see the blanket move and it'll be alright.* I forced myself not to blink, not to miss it, and I looked so long my eyes teared up and I had to stop, but the blanket was absolutely still. But that wasn't enough. I had to do something else. So I did this thing I'm not proud of but I had to.

I reached out and touched her shoulder. Her skin was cool, like she'd been sitting in some air-conditioned movie. I shook her. Nothing. Then—okay, I'll tell you—I took my pocket knife, that Swiss army thing you gave me for Hanukkah, and I opened the corkscrew part and I—touched her. Gently at first, a poke. Then harder. *Wake up, tell me there's nothing to be afraid of.* Nothing happened. I put the blade to her skin. I pressed. *Come on, come on.* Nothing. I dug, for chrissake I drew blood. *Come on!* I think I even shouted this time; thank God nobody heard me, nobody saw me, they would have dragged me away. But the point, sweetheart, is: nothing happened. And I understood what the nurse meant. This wasn't my mother, it wasn't anything; it was just a cold, empty piece of—stuff. There wasn't a damned thing I could do but I was still there. I heard a PA from the hallway: "Dr Mumblemumble, line 3," and I was still there. She was gone, things went on, and I was still there. See? There's nothing to be afraid of. It's only death. So, come, trust me. We'll find a way to be alone and you'll see. Take the knife. Grandma won't be there, grandma won't mind.

Take the knife. Please.

That's my boy.

###

BRIDGET, the Explorer

Ladies and Gentlemen: first of all, let me thank you. To be awarded the Golden Astrolabe award by the International Explorers Association is an honor I never thought I would achieve. Often, as a child, I would browse through my father's copies of your wonderful quarterly, *Whither Thou Goest?*, and pore over every page. And when I slept, I dreamt of amazing worlds to explore. That's how I first learned the legend of El Dorado.

El Dorado. Imagine it with me: that exotic city, hidden in the mountains of Peru, where the streets are paved with gold and the people all live in beauty and peace. In *Paradise Lost*, Milton tells us how the archangel Michael shows it to Adam. In *Candide*, Voltaire writes that people there live to great old age and die at rest and where—by no means the least of his delights—Candide is waited upon by twenty virgins. And Edgar Allen Poe, of course, has immortalized the city in his haunting lyric that tells of the gallant knight who searches his whole life:

And as his strength
Failed him at length,
He met a pilgrim shadow.
"Shadow," said he,
"Where can it be,
This land of Eldorado?"

"Over the mountains
Of the moon,
Down in the valley of the Shadow,
Ride, boldly ride,"
The shade replied,
"If you seek for Eldorado."

Reading this at the age of thirteen, I believed every word. After all, we here know that every myth has its origin in some bit of history; indeed, is that not the very motto of this organization? "No Dream Too Fantastic." Our own colleagues have proven this: when Stephan Beckerman discovered the fountain of youth in the swamps of Australia; when Pietro Dominico dug the Holy Grail out of a tar pit in New Mexico? So I vowed that I would also turn myth to history as well.

And, of course, I found it. Which is why we're all here. "To Bridget Hemisphere, for the Discovery of 'El Dorado.' One More Light against the Darkness." I will treasure this always.

Now, many of you have asked me to talk about my search. I have been offered small fortunes to tell how I found it, and I have always refused. The result is that my silence has been read as suspicious. Many of you even doubted that I'd actually succeeded. I've read the letters calling me a fraud who should be hanged at dawn.

But come, my colleagues: a little dose of reality here. Where would I have found the two golden robes I brought back? The centuries-old documents all examined and carbon-dated by experts? And the painting I stole, that Sotheby's itself has certified as authentic? Does it stand to reason I would fabricate my story, when it would be so easy to discredit me?

I'll tell you what it is, colleagues. Jealousy, pure and simple. Little Bridget Hemisphere, coming from nowhere, with no track record, her PhD not from Harvard but from Western Kansas State College. And, of course, lacking that most important of all qualifications for third-world exploration: a penis.

How else to explain all the efforts to stop me? Mr. Danielssen, our president, refused to allow me official sanction and support—so I had to get funds where I could. Can you imagine the absurdity of trekking through the mountains of Peru with "Walmart" written on our backs? Lord Henry Downing, chairman of our distinguished board, somehow never remembered to make that simple phone call to the Peruvian consulate for permission to cross their border, so that one-third of our measly funds went into bribery and extortion. And I won't even mention Miguel de Ojos del Lobo. The expert guide who just happened to lose his way for two weeks.

But why go on? It is clear that I triumphed in spite of your doubts and hostility. Nevertheless, as a sign that I bear no animosity, I will finally break my silence and tell you all exactly how I found the treasure city.

It was simple. The map was on a piece of scrimshaw that I found at a garage sale in Skokie, Illinois. Now of course you are all wondering how the location of an ancient city in South America would be known by a whaler from New England, and why he'd carve a map on a whale's tooth, and how *that* wound up outside Chicago and how my eyes just happened to fall on it as I was strolling past a very crowded table. Well, gentlemen, I could tell you it was fate, or luck, but I know such an answer would never satisfy you. Your masculine view of the universe has no room for such accidents. It takes a woman's mind to accept an act of faith as truth.

I see my time is running short. Senator Jim is spinning his finger. "Hurry up," he's saying, "I have to pee." Therefore I'll skip over the many details of the trip, how I found the one guide left alive who knew the way and just assure you that we found the place. So I come to the magical bridge.

There we were, on a bright summer morning. Facing us was a canyon so deep there was no way to get past it. But just beyond, on the other side we could see high golden towers sparkling in the light. My guide smiled at me. "Aqui," he said, "Aqui esta su ciudad." Yes, but how to get there? He whispered, "There is a bridge. It is called "El Camino Sueno." The Road of Dreams. It was invisible, but stretched across the canyon, wide enough and strong enough to bear any weight at all. You could not see this bridge. You could not reach out with your hand to feel it. The only way to cross was to step off the rocks into what looked like empty air. You either committed an act of faith and achieved your dream, or you stayed where you were as your heart broke.

My people begged me not to take the risk, but I had no choice. My life had led me up to this moment, and so I held my breath and took a quiet step off the rock. And, of course, it was true. There was a bridge, just as he said. I cried, I laughed, I danced, I don't know what I actually did, but before I knew it, there I was, on the other side, looking down into the fabled city.

And, oh my friends, it was everything it was promised to be. All described for you in my book. I stayed there for a month, and returned with the results that you know. With this honor bestowed upon me. The first woman in our history to be granted this plaque. What a pity, however, that tonight must be tarnished by controversy and ill-will. So, even though my time is running short, I must conclude with one more point. Senator Jim will have to cross his legs for another five minutes.

My point is simply this: My critics may actually be right. This award may be a farce after all. My search for El Dorado could easily have ended in failure and I could have forged all the evidence. The golden robes might easily have been lent to me from the collection of Baroness Elisabeth von Rothschild, my real patroness. The maps and papers might have been forged by scholars such as Carmen Maria Suarez, Gabrielle Dominique, or Esther Bernstein—all colleagues of mine. The carbon dating might have been fabricated by Bei Dan Chen, who heads the Beijing Archeological Laboratories. And the painting? Created by Dianna Becker, whose one-woman show has just won her a McArthur Genius grant.

All of whom, you notice, are women.

So there's a great possibility I may have caught all of you with your highly testosterone-laden pants down and embarrassed the shit out of this whole organization.

Or my story may be completely true after all. How will you know? You may not. You may just have to take the whole thing as . . . oh my gosh . . . an act of faith.

###

NORA, the Pedestrian

I try to walk at least a mile every day. Rain or shine, I put on my walking shoes with the jingle bells on them—I put the bells on because they make walking like music. I'll hum a song while those silver bells mark time. Sometimes it's a waltz: STEP-step-step, STEP-step-step. Sometimes I do a polka. Step-step-step-AND; step-step-step-AND. People look at me oddly; "Stay away; that one's looney." Well, sometimes it's good to be looney.

I've been doing this since the car accident, about three years ago. They said I'd never walk again, but I wasn't going to believe that. My parents taught me if you put your mind to it, if you put your heart and soul to work, you could do anything! So as soon as I could, I got out of that wheelchair and started walking.

First I just walked around the bed. That was the first hurdle, the psychological one. Then I forced myself to walk to the bathroom on my own. You can't imagine the sheer delight of being able to use the toilet all by yourself. And then I went up and down the street, then around the block, then around a different block—a little bit more every day until now I go for hours and never get tired.

I've made some wonderful friends on my walks. Simone, the cocker spaniel, who runs to the fence so I can pet her. Abercrombie, the big old German shepherd, who, believe it or not, actually barks in rhythm. He hears my jingle bells coming down the street and joins right in. And of course interesting people. Old Mr. Coldwell, out no matter what the weather. He won't stop and talk, but we huff and puff together as we pass each other. There's Mollie Jackson, walking her baby. And, my favorites: the girl and her little brother, waiting on the corner for the school bus. I've watched them grow older; first she held his hand, then he wouldn't let her, and then he wouldn't even stand next to her, and now, it's so wonderful—they holds hands again.

And so it goes. Every day, as I said, until, you can imagine, it started to become dull.

So I started exploring. Instead of turning east on Meredith Lane, I'd go west. Or north on Farwell. One block farther each week. They said I'd never walk again, but oh, what wonders I saw!

First there was the garden. A half mile west of the Dairy Queen, behind the drive-in car wash, there's a lovely old Victorian house on a quarter acre of land. It's fenced in, of course, but through the slats I can see roses and day lilies and a lovely pebbled walk that leads somewhere I couldn't see. I imagine myself like Alice, skipping into some private Wonderland of my own.

Then the cemetery. About three miles northwest of Marcie's Salon, north on Sycamore. I wander among the old graves, with their headstones standing proudly against the ravages of time. Some of them are still legible: Ethan Stratford, 1845—1908. John and Martha Cunningham, Beloved through Eternity. Private Joshua Welles, Company D, Army of the Potomac, 1845—1863. It made me grateful just to be alive.

But the best day of all, of course, is when I found the circus.

I stumbled upon it by accident, out where the suitcase factory used to be before they tore it down. An actual circus, yes, like in picture books. A big tent with pennants whipping in the breeze. Game booths and sideshows and popcorn stands. Clowns putting on their makeup; trainers putting the elephants through their paces; a young man doing acrobatic warm-ups: the sword swallower, I was in heaven!

Then I heard music coming from the main tent, and so I peeked in, and there they were: the tightrope walkers. Two men working around this steel wire that was stretched just off the ground, I guess for practice. The younger man was on the wire, walking forward very slowly. His teacher was coaching him: "One step at a time, don't think about the ground, focus your eyes on the spot. Okay. Now, do it." And all of a sudden the young man stopped, he bent down just a little and-lord have mercy!-he jumped right up in the air, did a flip-flop backwards, and then landed smack dab back on the rope without blinking an eye. He grinned at himself, threw up his arms in a victory salute: "Ta-DAAAHHH!"

And before I could stop myself, I started applauding. "Hooray!" And they turned and saw me. I blushed: "I didn't mean to interrupt, but that was splendid!" They came over and shook my hand and we introduced ourselves and we chatted, and—oh, my lord, I can hardly believe what happened next.

The older one said, "Would you like to try it?" And without breaking a heartbeat I said, "Of course." So they took me over to the wire; they had me take my shoes off and then carefully helped me up onto it. "Find the center," he said; "You have to find the meridian of your sole." He meant "sole" like in shoe, but he could just as well have meant "soul" like inside your very heart. Because at the bottom, that's what it's really all about. And they got me balanced, each holding one hand. "Now, lift your right foot slowly, keeping your concentration on your left meridian. You won't fall; we're here. Now put your right foot down, find the meridian. Good. Now lift your left." And so on, gently guiding me halfway down the wire. And then they let go of my hands and said, "Now you're on your own. Finish the walk!" And my heart nearly stopped but I did it. I actually walked the whole tightrope! And as I'm doing it, I'm thinking of all those people who said I'd never walk again; if they could see me—

Hello? Hello? Oh, Harriet, I didn't hear you come in. No, I was just sitting here, talking to myself. But you came just in time. My bag is full and I need to use the toilet; can you wheel me over and help me get on it?

###

55

ALYSON, the Grown-up

(NOTE: This is a text message that Alyson, a teenager, is sending to her girlfriend. It is to be spoken one symbol, word, or letter at a time. Capital letters in clusters are to be read as phrases that belong together and read as one word. Thus: OMG is read as "ohemgee." "Space" is exactly that: a space between one word and the next. Letters grouped together in Caps that look like words are not to be read as words but spelled out, each letter separated. Thus DID is spoken as Dee Eye Dee.)

OMG space 2 AWSM space I space D I D space I T space ME &YKW space M space I N space H S space B T H R M space N O W space H S space P space OOT space H space S Y S space I space 456wKOTLS space LH6s space MELOL space R space U space OYFM question space H space I space M space 2 space H A R D space H R T S exclamation point space M space TMI space WTMI space H space I space S R I U S space I space 456U4EVR space M space W space U space 456 space M E space T M R O W question. H space YS space I space W L space M R Y space U space L A T R space M E LOL space H E LOL 2 space W E space B T H space NU space BS space 2 space rxs space T H E N space MOR space KOTL & space T H E N space H space T C H E D space M E space SFA space H space S O O N R space R space L T R space Y space N O T space N O W question space I space T C H space H I S space YKW space I T space FNY space H space S M B D Y space Y space N O T space M E question space M space YES space W E space D I D space I T space N O T space H U R T space 2G2BT space H space K N K N G space 2s space C U T M R W space YR G U B G

(This is what it means:
Oh my god. Too awesome. I did it. Me and you know who. I'm in his bathroom now. His parents are out of town. He says I love you with kisses on the lips. Let's have sex Me, laughing out loud. Are you out of your freaking mind? Him, I am too hard it hurts! Me, too much information. Way too much information. Him, I'm serious. I love you forever. Me, will you love me tomorrow? Him, yes. I will marry you later. Me, laughing out loud. Him, laughing out loud too. We both knew it was bull shit. Too much drugs. Then more kisses on the lips and then he touched me. So freaking awesome. Him, sooner or later; why not now? I touched his you know what. It was funny. Him, somebody; why not me? Me, yes. We did it. It didn't hurt. It was too good to be true. Him knocking. Time for seconds. See you tomorrow, Your grownup best girlfriend.)

###

ETHEL, the Acupuncturist

Just a few more, honey, and then I'll let you rest. That's the trick with needles; you gotta give 'em time to do their work. So where was I? Oh, yeah, the new television set.

So I says, "Teddie, for chrissake! I bought it; get used to it!" What a cheapskate. And what a control freak. Men, don't get me started. You married? Yeah, I see the ring. Don't move. The needles don't work if you move around too much. Just lay still. Just a few more.

I says to him, we should buy the best. Flatscreen digital is the new technology; what are we, cave people or something? I mean, I finally got him to buy a decent cable package, and he sits there owning the remote. God forbid that I, little powerless stupid *woman* that I am, should ever once get my hand on that remote! You'd think it was his freaking willie. What is it with men? Give 'em a phallic symbol and they go prehistoric.

Don't move, honey. I'm gonna put a couple on your feet. Most people don't let me get near their toes, but really your feet are the most important parts of your body. Every channel of energy that runs through your body, it's got a point on a foot. Like you feel this point here? Where else do you feel something? Right, yeah; right there on top of your ear! You wouldn't think so but—oh, sorry. I pressed too hard, I got carried away. You're getting tense again. No worry, everybody, their first time with acupuncture, it takes getting used to.

We don't reuse them, no. We don't send them away to be sterilized and recycled. Here; see? Disposable toxic waste, it's written right there on the lid. Trust me. I wouldn't be in business if I didn't know what I was doing, honey. Besides, your friend Margaret who recommended me, she's alive and kicking, right? No tetanus there; no rigor mortis— honey, I'm just joking with you.

Honey, don't go tense like that; I can tell, you're clenching your jaw so tight you're gonna have your bottom teeth coming out of your eyes. Let's try this, okay? When I say breathe in, you breathe in, and then let it out in a slow whooooooosshh, like that. Try it. In . . . hold . . . whooooosh. Good. You're doing great. Keep breathing.

So anyhow, Teddie, he starts giving me grief. "It's for the house; when we buy something for the house, we buy it together." Yeah, right; except he was out of town, it was a one-day New Year closeout. So finally, I looked him in the eye. Always look 'em right in the eye, they're like dogs, they always have to blink first. And I says, I say "Teddie, get off your toilet, okay? You're pissed because I paid what I paid or you're pissed because I went over your freaking head and made a decision on my own?"

Oh, sorry, sorry, sorry. Here, lemme put some alcohol on that. That's why it's important you don't move. Keep breathing. You're doing it wrong. You have to go OUT before you can go IN. It's not OUT, IN; it's IN, OUT.

So he goes and takes it back. Just for show, just to prove his stupid point. So now we're back to square one. Well, you know what'll happen? He'll be smug and all "big-man-in-control" for a while and then it'll be time for the freaking Super Bowl, and Sears will have another once-in-a-lifetime sale, and he'll go out and buy one, bigger than the one I got, it'll have twice as many bells and whistles, it'll be a god-damn space station in our living room, and he'll say "You see? If you'd'a waited a little longer, they'd've all come down. Women just don't know how to shop."

And I'll nod and agree with him, because what he don't know is that this is exactly what I planned on. I knew they were coming down in price. I knew he'd never get his fat ass around to buying one, him riding the buffalo and all that, and I'd have to make the first move.

There. That's the last one. Now, lemme just give these a little hum to get the energy flowing. Try to relax, honey. You gotta work with the needles, work with the needles. Now come on, close your eyes. I'll dim the light, it'll be nice and cozy. Good. Now, breathe. Breathe in, come on. . . . Good. Keep it up. Take yourself to your happy place. You gotta have some place in your life that's yours, that makes you happy, you know what I mean? A brook? A forest? Ah, then your favorite chair it is, with some great book. "The Mist of Avalon?" Never heard of it, but whatever it takes, just keep your eyes closed. Think about the room, the chair you're in, the book. Good. The house is quiet, the kids are all at school. Okay you don't have kids but get yourself *someplace*, honey; the needles don't work by themselves.

That's better, that's more like it. Make like your body is a big ice cube and it's melting. Now, I'm gonna just tweak them all a little bit, to get the chi flowing. In a little while, you'll feel all that blocked-up chi just flowing like a summer brook going downstream. Don't think about anything. Like I was saying, the freaking television set: I had to make the first move or we'd be living in the stone age. That's how you treat men, am I right or am I right?

(Lights slowly fade as SHE fades out, still talking.)
I mean, men may think they're the thing because they grow whiskers and fart, but when it comes to being smart . . . just relax, honey, your breathing's getting a little tense again. . . . Where was I? Oh, yeah, the television set.

###

ARTIE, the Single Girl

Hey. . . . How're you doing? . . . Crowded tonight. . . . I think it's the holidays; they make everybody really sociable. You come to these things a lot? Oh, god, that didn't come out like I meant, it's not that you look like some pathetic loser who has to come to these mixers to meet somebody, like you were some kind of—I'm making it worse. I have dug myself into a deep hole of bullshit, and I will never be able to dig myself out.

. . . Ah, you're smiling. I never know how to start, you know? Some women are good at this. Me, I been sitting for half an hour, trying to think clever and then so I thought just go over there and say something. What's the worst that could happen? You walk away, right? I mean, we all get rejected once in a while and I just did it again, didn't I? Should I just give up now? I mean, if I stuffed my big mouth with some more shrimp dip, there'd be no room for my foot. Or you could go over there and talk with that redhead you came in with and you could laugh about this sad case who made a fool of herself, and meantime I'll go home, watch some Netflix or some more Marion Zimmer Bradley. Do you like lesbian fantasy? My ex, she used to say, "Lesbianism is already a fantasy," which I thought was pretty bitchy of her at the time, but lately I think maybe she had a point. We have these illusions, you know, of what love should be like, I mean, maybe not even love, but just somebody you can piss off once in a while and she'll still be your friend, or like somebody you can call at two in the morning when it's scary. I know: you're waiting for me to take a breath so you can get a word in, but I'm afraid the word's gonna be "I came in with my lover, and I think she's waving at me like she wants to leave, it was nice talking with you." Now you're chuckling, well, I'm making progress. Have some shrimp dip.

. . . I'm trying to be an architect. . . . Yes, you're right: you don't hear a lot about women architects, most of the famous ones are men, but, I mean, like who designed the Viet Nam memorial? That was a woman. I mean, I could rattle off a half dozen names of women you probably never heard of, and that's because all the good commissions, the high-profile jobs, they always go to men. It's like orchestra conductors, you don't hear a lot about women conductors. Or plumbers. Or commercial pilots. The men have it all sewn up. It figures, don't it? What do architects build? Skyscrapers. What do conductors use? These little sticks. Skyscrapers. Pipes. It's all in the phallic symbol, it's all in the dick. I wrote that on one of my applications to school. I said, "It's time the dick was taken out of the art of the building." Of course I didn't get in: the admissions officer was a guy. Worse, his first name was Peter.

. . . Yeah, I know. I get wound up. But small talk? There I'm no good. I think it's how you were raised, don't you? I mean, like, some people are raised in households where everybody talks all the time. Yadda yadda blah blah, they just go on. Like Sandra, one of my ex-es. I went to her house and I could see where she got it. We were having chicken, and her mom and her dad and her kid sister, they spent the whole supper talking about chicken: what's the best way to cook 'em, do you buy 'em free range or frozen, her Mom's friend keeps kosher and what's that all about. But at my house, dinner was like a funeral. "Good chicken. Huh." So I grew up in silence. It was scary. When people are always quiet, you never know what they're thinking; they could be thinking, hey what a dork she is, or hey I love her or hey I gotta go to the bathroom, so you never know where you stand. And so then when you have something really important to talk about, they don't know how to take it. Like when you bring home a report card and it's all "A's"—because some of us are good at that, you know; some of us don't have a lot of real-world skills but we're very good in school—they don't say "Wow, great job!" Instead they say, "Huh. Where do I sign?" Or when you make the girl's basketball team, which where I come from is really hard to do, but you never get "Way to go, supergirl!" All you get is "Girl's basketball ain't the same; it's sissy stuff." Or when you take the deep plunge and try to have the really big conversation, the one about coming out, which is not easy for some of us, they don't say, "We love you and support you and, hey, we want you to be happy blah blah." No. He says, "Don't come around here anymore." And when you call to wish them Merry Christmas, he won't even take your phone call. So that's what I'm saying. Those things happen. It's no wonder you're not good at talking to people. Which is why I hate mixers. I do better online. Online I'm funny and smart and I make a very good impression, but as soon as we get face to face, I freeze up. I think it's because we're looking at each other, right? I say something and I can see your reaction; I can see you looking around the room or at your drink or over my shoulder—just like that—and I'm thinking, "How am I fucking up this time?" Which may or may not be the truth; for all I know you could be having lesbian fantasies about me and who knows what—but I'm not used to it. It's all that silence again. So maybe, like my counselor says, I shouldn't look at the people I'm talking to so I don't see their reaction, which sounds pretty stupid when you think about it because you're putting that person in the same position you hate being in, or maybe, like she says, I should ask. Yeah, like, "Am I boring you?" Because what's the other person gonna say? "Yes, you're boring the fucking shit out of me, you pathetic sad unhappy dyke. You got issues; get over it and move on." Which is why I been trying for the last thirty really nerve-wracking minutes to think up something clever to say.

. . . Oh. Yeah. She IS your lover, right. . . . So, like, nice talking to you.
    (SHE looks around, approaches another person.)
. . . Hey. Hi. How're you doing? Crowded in here tonight.
    (LIGHTS FADE as SHE continues to talk:)
I think it's the holidays. I love the holidays, you know what I mean, they make people like really sociable. It's a great time to meet new people . . . .

###

CONSTANCE, the Career Girl

No, I don't mind. I get asked that question a lot. We've got some time before my speech.

To start off with, you have to know that my dad is a dick. And I'm not just saying that because I hate him. You ask anybody who knows him. Especially my mom, if you could catch her sober.

Probably because he expected a boy. Not so much a son as maybe a second chance. I mean, most reasons guys want sons is to make up for the failures of their own lives; they make sure their sons do all the things they were too lame, too scared, too pathetic to ever do themselves. So when they get a daughter, they have to think outside the box. At least the Good Dads do. They get over their disappointment and grow up. Sometimes, like when she gets dressed up for the prom, or gets married, they even like it.

But DickDads never get over their disappointment and they try to make their daughters into sons. When that happens, you have only one choice: to fight back.

Starting with the tumbling lessons, which I hated. Doing round-off flip-flops, getting on the balance beam, it all scared the shit out of me, but every time I protested, he'd chew me out. "You're a pathetic loser, you make me sick." This to a ten-year-old. So the night before the state finals, I took half a dozen of Mom's allergy meds in vinegar water and vomited myself out of the running. He didn't talk to me for days.

He even ruined Halloween; I wanted to be Sleeping Beauty, this costume I'd seen in Walgreen's, with the lace and the ribbons, the flowing skirt, all so feminine, but nope. I had to be a pirate. I argued "There weren't any lady pirates!" But he dragged me to my computer and made me google "Female Pirates" and then he made me dress up as Anne Bonney in his old hunting outfit with the stained mud pants and the hip-boots. He stuck a black patch over my eye and painted a freaking MOUSTACHE on my upper lip. Well, I had planned in advance. I didn't pee for the whole afternoon and let go in those pants. I don't think he ever wore them again.

High school clubs? Spring musical? No. I had to play basketball, but I fouled out in every single game I played. He never caught on; he just thought I was a klutz and hated me even more.

But we had our biggest fight over my college major. I wanted to go into theater. Dad insisted I major in business so I could come into the firm. It was going to be Burkhart and Son even if the son had boobs. When I protested, it was my life after all, he said okay, I could major in whatever I wanted, but if it wasn't business he wasn't gonna pay the bill. And I told him, fine: I'd work my way, I could do it, I could do anything. And my freshman year I held down two part-time jobs and got a half-way decent scholarship. But what happened was, of course, that since I was working so hard I couldn't be in any school plays. And I couldn't get any decent homework time, so my grades sucked. Which of course made His Supreme Dickness very happy. So finally I had to give in. I switched back to business and played by his rules.

But of course the King of Dicks kept adding to the rules. Every summer when I had time, so I could've auditioned at the community theater we had, I had to intern in his office, dressing up in a suit and following him around all day. He didn't give me anything to do, mind you. I just filed and answered the phone and made coffee. That seemed all I was good for. That was the killer part: he just never trusted me.

No, wait. The killer part is the day he chewed into Betty, this girl on his staff, a smart, nice kid in marketing. I don't know what she screwed up on but suddenly, right there, at this weekly meeting we had, he tore into her like a Nazi. She was dumb, stupid, she had no business being in a man's world, all she had the brains for was to be a cocktail wait-ress or an airline stewardess and more daggers like that and I could see her across the table from me, staring at the dick, trying to hold it together while he ranted on. I waited for her to get up and walk out like a human being. But no: she sat there and took it. And I knew how to get back at him.

So I played his game. I switched my major. I pumped my GPA up to 3.8. I ran the stu-dent council. I joined the Junior Executive Club. I graduated magna cum laude and went on to grad school and I now have an MBA. I am eminently qualified to start up a new business with my eyes closed. I know how to read market plans and figure long-range strategies; I can negotiate with assholes and win every time; I can turn your failing dream into a blue-chip success within five years. I could be earning six figures from my consult-ing fees alone. In short, I made sure the hundreds of thousands of dollars Daddy shelled out for my education was very well worth it. He got his money's worth. Every dick-head penny.

But the best part was seeing his face when I told him my career plan. How I was going to spend the rest of my working life. What use I was going to make of that small fortune he spent on me.

Oh, but I gotta go. I gotta make my announcement.

Ladies and gentlemen: the captain has turned on the seat-belt sign in preparation for landing. At this time, please be sure your seat backs are in their upright positions and your trays are locked. I'll be passing
      (LIGHTS start to fade.)
down the aisle to pick up any glasses or cans you might have. On behalf of the crew, I want to thank you for flying with us today, I hope the next time you have occasion to travel the skies, you'll think of us. . . .

###

MARCIA, the Diver

I am so glad I found this website, truly. I need advice. I am a transgender person. It's funny that when you say it, it's easy enough, but when you write it down, does THAT take nerve.

Like most of you, I was born a man but I know that was a mistake. I knew the first time my mom and me played dress-up and we put polish on my toenails. I'm sure she knew; she told me, "Mark, you only get one chance in this world. Don't screw it up." Well, it wasn't me that screwed up. *God* screwed up. Somehow I got over the worst parts, like being teased in school because I couldn't toss a baseball. Like having to deal with shaving that ugly hair off my face. Like not caring when salespeople look at me funny when I try on heels. Like having to look at and deal with that thing between my legs. Like not having a social life ever, not to mention a sex life. Well, if you're reading this, you been there. So I been saving money regular for some time now and I'm, like six, seven months away from the thirty-fivegrand I need. So you wouldn't think I have a problem. But here it is.

For about six months now, I been dating a great guy. He only knows me as Marcia. We met at a church potluck. So I haven't told him about my "man" parts yet. I haven't had to, if you know what I mean. He's kind of a religious guy, so he thinks we shouldn't have sex until we're both really sure we want to. You gotta love a guy like that. But after a while, he started making like he thought it was time and so we started fooling around. I gave him oral and things like that. So far, so good.

Then one night we're walking in the mall and there's these two guys walking together holding hands. He said "That's disgusting, it makes me sick. They oughta arrest people like that." I shoulda said something then and there, but I couldn't. Then another time we went to this new club to try it out only we didn't know it was "gay and lesbian night." We were dancing, and some guys, they started dancing around us, fooling around, and then two guys tried to sandwich him and suddenly he blows up. He starts swearing. The other guy answers back. My friend then punches him! The whole club is watching and the owner starts over and so I grab my friend's arm and hauled ass outa there. But all the way home, he kept on about it: "Perverts. Disgusting. They have no morals; they're sinning against the Bible, and on like that and my stomach's turning somersaults and I want to throw up."

So, like I said, I'm in spitting distance of the operations and so I keep thinking maybe I could keep things like they are for a while and never have to tell him. But now I'm starting to get scared. Who knows what he could do?

One time, I almost got caught. He spent the night over, I made him sleep on the couch and he got a little annoyed but it was okay. But there I was in the shower and he was trying to get in there with me, but I had the shower door locked and I told him no because I was shaving down there and didn't want him to see, and he said okay but he'd wait anyhow so he could finally get to see me naked. But I had this big bath towel so I put that on and made some joke about needing to be a good girl for Santa Claus and he laughed and asked if I had, like, varicose veins or something? I knew he was faking it, and his patience was wearing out.

63

Because last night he laid down the law. He said like it's been six months and how bad do I want to have sex with him. He says he's getting all tense about it and wasn't it time and didn't we care about each other. And all this while he was kissing me all over and started to try to finger me. I took his hand and put it over his crotch and got down and gave him oral and so he didn't follow up on it. But I know he will.

So I don't know what to do. I know what people are gonna say because I been saying it to myself a long time now. I have to respect myself. I have to live my own life. If I love him, I should tell him and if he loves me, he'll be okay with it because love should be unconditional. Well, "should-be's" don't cut it out in the real world.

What I need to do is go ahead and get the surgery and figure out a way to explain why I'm out of touch for a while But my doctor ain't available for another 4 months and I don't have the money yet. There is another doctor I heard of who will do the job next month and is fifteen grand cheaper but I've heard horror stories about him being a back-alley quack and that scares me.

Or else I need to break up with this guy. Stand up for myself, show him. Lift up my skirt one time and show him what's hanging there. Yeah, and I know who'd get tossed two feet across the room THAT time.

You see the place I'm in? Either way I go, I'm scared. How did I let myself get in this mess in the first place? It's the diving board. One time I was on the diving board and I was scared to jump and there was this line behind me jeering and calling me names. And my Mom hollered up, "Darling, you gotta go one way or the other cuz you can't stand still!" Boy, if she were around, I bet she'd—.

But wait, wait. I just had a thought. Something else my Mom used to say. Yes. And she was right. Now I know what I'm gonna do. I don't really have any choice.

So wish me luck, readers. Wish me luck. Oh, and one thing more. Pray for me too.

###

ALEXANDRA, the Music Lover

Oh, darling, I'm so sorry to hear about you and Travis. But he wasn't good for you and you know it. . . . Me and Richard? There's no secret, it's all very simple. It's Bach. Yes, the composer. He has all the answers, the world makes perfect sense once you understand him. I mean all those cantatas, the masses—Lord, the first five minutes of the "Magnificat" alone have so much to say about the meaning of life, the structure of the universe, the whole gestalt of mankind's yearnings and accomplishments at one and the same time.

That's what I do when it gets to be too much. Just the other day, Gretchen was after me on the Brewster campaign: the client pushed the meeting up a day and wanted to see a few extra layouts "just in case." It was already 3:30, my migraine was setting a new world record and the kitchen was out of Milky Ways, so I put on my headset and cranked up Christopher Parkening on Cantata 147.

(SHE hums "Jesu, Joy of Man's Desiring.")

Three minutes later, the image came to me, and once you get the image, the rest is just scribbling. There's Richard, smiling at me.

(SHE waves and calls to him.)

Happy anniversary to you too, sweetheart!

(Back to her conversation.)

He knows what we're talking about. He doesn't believe it, but he puts up with me anyhow.

But I didn't always understand this. I came to Bach late in life, having spent my youth on the latest boy group at first, then folk rock, and then easy listening. So I didn't know much about classical music, except that Beethoven was deaf, Brahms wrote a lullaby and Mendelssohn invented weddings. I was *Classical Music for Dummies* live and in person.

Then Richard, when we were dating, won a pair of tickets to hear "The St. Matthew Passion" and persuaded me to go with him. I don't know why I said I would; probably because he was so great in bed and why would I risk that? So there I was, in Orchestra Hall listening to sounds I'd never heard before, and by the time they got to the final chorus, "Wir setzen uns mit," I was transformed. The sound, the texture, the depth. I thought at the time it must be like what deep-sea divers experience a mile under: dark, endless, beautiful.

Remember: until then, my life was like yours. Chores, deadlines, meals, job insecurity, and not making waves. There was no center, no discernable sense or logic to it. None of that intelligence and order that's at the core of every piece Bach ever wrote: the intricacies, the structures of the fugues, the variations around the obscure but ever present core. I mean, take the score for "The Goldberg Variations." Open it to any page and follow the notes going up, down, circling around, in some mad frenzied cacophony, that one simple phrase where all the meaning lies. It must be how God sees the universe: all the stars, the planets, the black hole: every conceivable thing, dancing some lunatic quadrille around a gigantic metaphorical maypole set smack dab in the middle of it all.

I'm not making any sense. How can you put into words something so vast and yet so simple? Just listen to the "Toccata and Fugue." It's all there. No wonder Einstein played him to relax. And I wondered if life isn't like that. Was Bach reflecting the world as he saw it in his baroque way, or was he only imagining the *possibilities* that would accrue if we could only find the core of our lives as easily as we find the core of a song in C Major? If life were only as clear as "Sleepers Awake."

(SHE hums a bit of that.)

And then I thought: Maybe at the bottom, it really is. I mean, if we sat down and wrote out a chart of our days, wouldn't there be a pattern? Some coherence at the deep core of it all? I mean, you talk to priests or nuns and they'll tell you it's God. Or you talk to physicists and they'll give you string theory, while geneticists talk about DNA bar coding. Everybody's searching for a center; so why couldn't it be a diminished fifth g-minor chord?

I set out to make mine just that; to become, as it were, the "Second Brandenburg Concerto" on two legs. I bought books. I took classes. I joined endless Bach societies and Facebook pages. I bought a keyboard and started taking lessons: I can now play the "Minuet in G."

(SHE plays a couple bars on air piano as SHE hums the melody.)

Richard understands perfectly. After all, this is our tenth anniversary and what does that tell you? He's the tonal center in the double fugue of my life. I think the Gershwin boys had it almost right. I have Richard and I have Bach: who could ask for anything more?

###

BARBARA, the Swimmer

Oh, God, I can't swim! I'm going to drown, Kick. Help! Help! Nobody. They all went down,. I don't want to drown. Oh God! Billy, if you can—He's been dead years; yes: they say you go mad before you drown, you fight and then go mad and give in; you just have to fight being afraid. Kick, kick. We were laughing, there was no sign at all, the wave, the wind, no warning and they're all dead. Oh, God, please don't make me afraid. Here comes another wave. Ride the wave, hold your breath, as long as you can keep your head up, oh God, I'm under, it's dark, brown, grey, no light, where's the surface, you'll die of cold, the *Titanic* people froze to death. Look: there's the sky, so near so far!

(Breathing each breath sharp and urgent.)

hoh, hoh, hoh, hoh, Kick. I can't go down again, you go down three times you're dead. Relax. Save your energy. Use your arms, snow angels, Grandpa's backyard, great big wings and Rita's were bigger but yours were smoother and then you laid in the dog poop and Grandma was mad when you trekked dog poop into the front room and it's freezing like that now, my arms are getting numb. Oh Jesus, another big wave, don't fight it, you'll get tired, I'm dreaming, a nightmare I'll wake up. Billy, I'm sorry I lied, I love you, help me. I should have told you before the accident. God I can't feel my legs, kick! It's not doing any good, it's so cold. Ride the wave, don't go down; it's so dark, close, there are things in the water, dark things coming toward me, which way do I kick, where's the surface? I can't make it, yes you can. I won first prize didn't I? The Centennial Pool Junior Dolphins Dunking-and-Hold-Your-Breath-Contest, I won first prize for forty-five seconds, I tried for forty-six but I couldn't do it, but I beat Cissy that's all that counted. *Hoh, hoh, hoh!* Billy. I don't believe in God but maybe I'm wrong; Billy, make the waves stop.

Oh Jesus. Billy believed more than I did, he always liked to think he was holy, but even a holy man, even a priest sometimes gives in and forgives. I'm sorry I cheated. I'm sorry I went with David; forgive me, stop the waves, Why do I deserve this? You should die fast, I could let go, relax, take one long breath, how long can it last. It's cold, I want to die warm, I don't want to die shriveled and cold, I'll look like a raisin when they fish me up; stop making jokes. Billy always hated when you made jokes; what did Jesus fart? No. Think on thy end, Oh, Man. Think not on the earth. Do angels fart? Even Jesus must have had diarrhea at least once.

Stop; don't go mad, you'll be fine. But you've been down twice already or was it just once? How many times did you go under? Is this life flashing like they say? Kick, you can, your arms are not tired, you can't go down the third time. In Spanish that would be *tres.*" Spain. How awful. The sun. Spencer hit on me and then he lied but Billy believed him. But there was justice; Spencer died in the war. Maybe there's justice in heaven. Billy won't let me die like this, he'll turn the other cheek—. Oh, God, there's that oar again; maybe I can get there. *Holy Mary full of grace, the lord is with thee, blessed art thou,* how the hell does it go? *Our father, who art in Heaven,* yeah, like that's gonna do any good; who the hell turned the boat over in the first place? Does God want me to drown? Are my sins so horrible, my lies and my cheating; does that mean I have to die this cold lonely death? *Kyrie Eleison, I believe in God, the Father almighty, creator of heaven and earth. I believe in Jesus Christ, his only Son, He was conceived by the power of the Holy Spirit and something and something and something and on the third day he rose again*—three, three times and I'll rise again, right? I'm choking, are you supposed to swallow water or spit it out. Is this the fourth? It's a lie then, I'll survive, it doesn't matter. It's dark. And there are things in the water, hands, there are hands in the water. Billy? Look up there, it's the sky, just out of reach, oh God if I could just reach the sky, I have to breathe, I don't care, Billy, there you are, there you are; give me your hand. . . . Billy, Billy, hold me. . . .

###

KATHRYN, the Patient

Dear Christine:

If you are reading this, it means I am dying. I'm probably asleep with a morphine drip in my arm, and I have been this way for several days now. Hopefully I'm at home, but knowing you as I do, how cautious, how bloody *careful* you are about everything, I'm probably in St. Mary's Hospital, with tubes and monitors attached to me everywhere. You've made me the bionic woman. Although, if you're anal-retentive, it's probably my fault for doing a bad job on your toilet training.

But I have a great favor to ask of you. Don't say "no" until you've read this entire letter twice. You're my only hope.

When I was sixteen, after my parents threw me a horrible party where they showed all my baby pictures, I swore to myself that nobody would ever be in charge of me but myself. I would run my life my own way. And so I wrote out a list of all the things I wanted to accomplish before I died.

I wanted to marry a wonderful man and share a good life with him. Which explains why I was divorced twice before I met your father. But when he came along, on our first date, he said the most gracious thing I ever heard and I knew he was Mr. Right. I won't tell you what he said, because it's none of your business. But he gave me forty years of wonder and delight.

I wanted to have lots of children, but as it turned out, you were the only one. But, believe me, you were—you ARE—a most wonderful daughter. Your sense of humor, your intelligence, your passion for doing everything, your total YOU-ness. One night, when he was where I pretty much am right now—dying, that is—he told me that you were, to him, every single child we couldn't have all rolled into one and he was more than satisfied. Me too, sweetheart. I am more than satisfied.

So that took care of my domestic life. I wrote down other goals for myself and kept a list with me all my life. Here they are in no particular order.

I have climbed Mount Rainier. I know it's not the tallest, but it was tall enough for me. Your father was along and somewhere we have a photograph of it. If you find it, I want you to save it and give it to my first granddaughter.

I entered the Illinois State Fair cake bake-off and won first prize, with Grandmom's carrot cake supreme recipe with coconut frosting. After I won the prize, I burned the recipe. No looking back, I said.

I bowled one perfect three hundred game, when I was president of the Happy Hookers Saturday League. I don't remember why we called ourselves hookers. The week after my perfect game, I quit the league. No looking back, remember?

I have walked on every Civil War battlefield in America. I did that for your father, because I wanted to make him happy. When we had done it all, he took me to Europe, a bonus I hadn't planned on. Which just goes to show you: you can't control everything.

I finished every crossword puzzle I ever started, although it often took me three days. I gave up on Sudoku after the first one; it didn't teach me anything.

I put a rose on your great-grandfather's grave in Arlington every single Memorial Day of my life, except this last one. I expect you to take over from now on.

I made love to a woman once, to see what it was like. I didn't like it, the smells were all wrong. If that shocks you, shame on you.

I visited a church of every denomination in the city of Chicago. That includes a synagogue, a Buddhist temple, a Mormon tabernacle (that was hard to find), a Baptist revival where I stood out like a sore thumb, and a snake handler's ceremony. I wanted to find out who was right. You want to know? They all were.

I taught myself to fix the toilet, the bathtub drain, the carburetor, the sump pump, and the lawnmower. I did every oil change on every car I ever owned.

I have run every Chicago marathon since they started. I never came in first, but never wanted to. If I'd wanted to, I would have.

There are more, but I'm getting tired. Here are some I missed out on.

I never learned to ride a horse, a camel, or a missionary.

I never learned to tap dance.

I never served on a jury. I was called dozens of times, but I just wasn't smart enough to play dumb.

I never learned to swim. I think that is the only thing I am ashamed to admit.

So. I think I've made my point. Now, the hard part.

If you are reading this, you are at my bedside, wherever it is. My breathing is irregular; I probably look like I'm gasping for breath. I have not eaten for over a week. Either they're feeding me liquid pablum through my arm or they're starving me. I have probably fouled myself at least once in this bed. I may have purple blotches all over my arms where they continue to poke me.

When, on one rare occasion or another, I am awake, I probably talk about the walls moving, hearing strange music, seeing your father on the TV screen, going down long tunnels, and who knows what. I probably have not spoken one decent word to you since I started climbing down the other side of the hill.

Now, please turn your attention to the morphine drip on my arm. Notice the mechanism, the device that controls the amount. For a while they were letting me administer it to myself, but I don't know how long since they took it out of my reach.

You have it in your hands. Turn it all the way as high as you can go. You've watched the nurse. You know how.

Yes, I want you to do that. If you believe in anything, and if I've raised you right, you'll do this for me. Turn the knob, sweetheart; I would do no less for you.

With all my love,

Mom.

###

ROSALIND, the Repeater

No, Betty, you're wrong. People DO live more than one life. They die and get born again and again. The Buddhists are right. No, I'm not just trying to cheer you up. I'm trying to give you some faith. Terminal cancer is not terminal, and there's nothing to be afraid of.

Me? Of course it happened to me. I've personally gone and come and gone and come again so many times it makes me dizzy to think. And that's just counting the times I remember.

Are you alright? Shall I call the nurse? I can barely hear you.

I know because it's all there, stored in your dreams and muscles. I mean, think about it; you've never ridden a horse, and yet you often dream of being on a black stallion storming through some distant surf. How did your imagination know how to ride like that? Or you may not remember living in Italy but you love all sorts of exotic pastas. Without your help, your taste buds are all singing Verdi.

Think about musicians or athletes or even when you type at your computer: none of that is conscious. The scales and the arpeggios, the windup and the pitch, where the "shift" key is: all of those are in your muscles, right? So, if the muscles contain all those complicated signals, doesn't it stand to reason they could contain signals from the past as well?

Or your fears. You're afraid of heights. I've seen it; you get above the fourth floor and you won't go near the windows. Clearly at least once you fell to your death. You never had a lesson but you're a natural swimmer; who taught you?

Me? Where to begin? I've been an African tribal princess. A priest in Atlantis—you note that deep water terrifies me. I was a soldier in the army of Henry the Fifth. I was a poor ignorant peasant in ancient China. I was Jane Austen: I was working on a new novel—called *The Brothers*—but the milk sickness took me too soon. They never did find the last chapters. When I came back next I wanted to finish it, but I was a slave in Virginia and never learned to write.

The best? There is no best; nor is there a worst. Lives are roller coasters, taking you up the mountain one time and down it another. As when I was in Henry's army. Yes, I was killed at Agincourt, but I had supper with the king the night before. He'd come, as Shakespeare has it, walking through the camps that night. He sat with us, told the dirtiest jokes I'd ever heard, and we laughed until dawn. Or when I was that Chinese peasant—I never had enough to eat or a dry place to dwell, but one day my sister's friend took me into a field and introduced me to the pleasures of love. I was ten and her name was Yu Lin: I don't know why I know that but somehow I do.

The best moment? You're going to force me to choose, aren't you? Very well.

I must have been ten years old at the time. My father herded sheep and oxen on a small piece of desert in the Middle East. I think I may have been the only child, but I can't be sure, because in the memory I have there were several of us, but somehow I'm sure I was the youngest. It was a warm spring night, I think, because I have no sensation of being cold or lonely or afraid. And the memory brings with it a smell of cooking. What were we doing? I thought I told you. We were watching the flocks; that's what shepherds do, even girl ones.

But I also think we were doing something illegal. There's a feeling in the memory of danger: maybe we'd slaughtered one of our fathers' lambs for our dinner, or maybe we were gambling with sticks, or maybe one of us was misbehaving with another. I don't know exactly what it was, but the air wasn't clear. Yes, there were stars a-plenty and a moon like a goose egg, but something wasn't right about the wind or the shifting molecules. I have this strange and awful sensation of drowning, and yet I was with my comrades at the top of the tallest hill there was.

And then one of us must have said something or pointed because we were all looking up at the stars. And they moved. The stars moved. It was like they were some sort of stage curtain strung across the universe and something was drawing the curtain aside, revealing to us a sort of universal stage where some monumental play was about to be performed. And then there was an angel. Yes. An angel. Well, perhaps you can anticipate the rest. It told us not to be afraid, for it had come with some very good news.

Well, of course you don't believe it. That's because you think it happened in December. The truth is nobody really knows when it happened. I did a lot of research because, well, you can imagine how amazing it was even to me! But it seems that years later, they picked December because they had to do something to make the unforgiving winter tolerable. But Christ could have been born in April for all that.

I don't remember any more details. I mean, I've pored over the gospels so many times to see if there were any mention of a young girl, but of course there isn't. And when I tell this story to priests or scholars, they laugh. By my muscles and dreams know what they saw.

So, don't be afraid. It doesn't matter how many times we die, so long as it's more than one.

Betty? Betty? Are you—?

Sleep well, Betty. I hope you come back a princess.

###

Epilogue

(Spoken by WOMAN or WOMEN)

So, my little one,

All potential and promise,

What have you seen?

Great joy or sorrow; all are here.

Satisfaction or regret; all are here.

But do not be afraid. Do not hesitate.

The only wrong choice you can make is to make none at all.

So be bold, little daughter, and come into the morning light.

Come. Choose.

(We) (I) await you.

###

Lightning Source UK Ltd.
Milton Keynes UK
UKOW03f0706020614

232690UK00002B/294/P